13

Downward Dogs & Warriors

Wisdom Tales for Modern Yogis

Downward Dogs & Warriors

Wisdom Tales for Modern Yogis

Zo Newell

HIMALAYAN
INSTITUTE®
PRESS

The Himalayan Institute Press
952 Bethany Turnpike
Honesdale, PA 18431 USA

www.HimalayanInstitute.org

13-ISBN: 978-0-89389-266-1
10-ISBN: 0-89389-266-1

Second Printing, 2007

Printed in Singapore

The paper used in this publication meets the minimum requirements of American National Standard of Information Sciences — Permanence of Paper for Printed Library Materials, ANSI Z39.48-1984.

Library of Congress Cataloging-in-Publication Data

Newell, Zo, 1950-
    Downward Dogs and Warriors: Wisdom Tales for Modern Yogis / Zo Newell.
        p. cm.
    Includes bibliographical references.
    ISBN-13: 978-0-89389-266-1 (alk. paper)
    ISBN-10: 0-89389-266-1 (alk. paper)
    1. Yoga. 2. Mythology, Indic.
I. Himalayan International Institute of Yoga Science & Philosophy.
II. Title.
    B132.Y6N44 2007
    181'.45--dc22   2007012735

Contents

Foreword

Like many other students, my first taste of yoga was learning the poses in an asana class. I fell in love with the shapes and sensations but was intrigued with the Sanskrit names as well. I began to read and study about yoga and enjoyed exploring the philosophy of this ancient art wherever I could find it. In the process I learned only bits and pieces about the origin of the asana names, but it was enough to understand that these powerful stories shaped the fabric of Indian culture from which yoga sprang.

So for two reasons I was pleased to read *Downward Dogs & Warriors*. First, it was a great delight to have so many of the stories behind the poses put together in one place and included in the format of practice. I also liked how each story was personified by a pose and, contrariwise, how each pose was connected to its story. As readers we can learn the story first and then discover the pose. Or, if we have already discovered the pose, we can deepen that discovery by reading the story that inspired it.

But the other reason I enjoyed the book was that I was especially moved by what Zo had written from her heart about her early life. I was fascinated and inspired by her personal story, how she had come to love and trust the wisdom of the stories, and how they had guided her through difficult periods during her growing-up years.

In *Downward Dogs & Warriors*, not only does Zo relate these oft-retold stories in a down-to-earth and clear way, she also adds a touch of her wit, so we are caught just enough off guard to remain present with the lessons we are receiving. She is gently adding to our wisdom just as her teacher taught her.

I first met Zo as a student in my yoga class, and over the years she has become a colleague and friend. I am always pleased to see her name on the list of students registered for a workshop, because I know she will contribute in many ways during the time she spends with her fellow students and me in the classroom. Blending insight and a bit of saucy wit, her soft Southern drawl may sometimes hide her sharp intelligence, but never her kind heart.

I heartily recommend this book to both beginners and seasoned practitioners alike. Pick it up and read the stories, then get on your yoga mat and embody them. The world will be a better place for it. Thank you, Zo, for this gift.

Judith Hanson Lasater, PhD, PT
San Francisco, June 2006

This book is dedicated to
the Highest of the High
and
to you, the reader.

Preface
How to Use This Book

There are many excellent books on how to do asana, but this is not one of them. This is a book about using asana and related images for reflection, self-examination, and healing. In it, I discuss the use of asana, mythology, and culturally resonant imagery as tools for deepening your yoga practice through observation of your body, your mind, and your emotions.

In the field of anthropology, *symbolic healing* refers to the deep structure that appears to underlie the universal experience of healing. This experience often occurs spontaneously in response to a particular myth or a psychologically true story. Individuals recognize, often on a very deep and non-intellectual level, that a particular story somehow "speaks" to their sense of suffering. Their emotions attach to symbols in the story; and as they hear the story, contemplate the emotionally significant symbol, and experience resolution along with the characters in the story, they experience a healing transformation of a personal dilemma.

Yoga philosophy takes it for granted that human life involves suffering, because we mistake the physical world and body for something of lasting spiritual value and significance. The practice of yoga, as explained by Patanjali (ca. 200 BCE) in the *Yoga Sutra,* is a process of dis-identifying with the body and things that change, and redirecting our sense of unity to the eternal and unchanging.

Patanjali identifies *svadhyaya,* self-study, as one of three key techniques in his system of kriya yoga. Traditionally, *svadhyaya* means the "going over" (*adhyayana*) of sacred texts such as the Veda or treatises on spiritual liberation, as well as the repetition of purifying prayers, such as the sacred syllable *Om.* This going over involves turning something over in the mind repeatedly, reciting something until it is memorized, learning it by heart, becoming or embodying it. Clearly, this is different from studying something for information or reading about a subject.

Michelangelo famously said that to sculpt a horse, he simply removed from the marble everything that was not the horse. In Patanjali's yoga, we have instructions on how to remove from consciousness everything that is not compatible with the enlightenment that is our natural state. We don't become someone else, someone enlightened; we become our most authentic self, which is to say, someone who is enlightenment itself, once our self-imposed beliefs in limitation are put into proper perspective.

It seems to me that the process of svadhyaya, the repeated, devoted return to a sacred text or prayer until it sings in our veins, includes a process of discriminating the part that—if you'll forgive my mixed metaphors—is the horse from the part that is not the horse. The more fully we embody the sacred teaching, the more easily we see what has to change or be discarded to make room for what we are becoming.

The third limb of Patanjali's yoga is *asana*, the physical dimension of yoga practice, and the one most familiar to Westerners. Through the practice of asana, we become increasingly conscious, not only of our physical bodies but also of our emotional and energetic dimensions. Asana is a mirror for self-awareness.

But the asanas we practice are only the tip of an enormous cultural and spiritual iceberg. The tip—the physical postures and their effect on our muscles, bones, circulation, and respiration—is so engaging in itself that, as yoga has become increasingly popular in the West, we seem to have lost sight, or awareness, of what lies beneath the surface. The rich artistic and mythological tradition of India, when brought into consciousness along with asana, transforms each pose into a lens through which we can discover hidden facets of, and possibilities for, ourselves. Together, the pose, the story, and the artistic image enlarge the power and range of our self-understanding; and it's been my experience that engaging with the poses, stories, and images can elicit a powerful experience of symbolic healing.

Physically, you need a true sense of where your body is misaligned if you are to correct it. In the beginning the teacher demonstrates the pose and, as the student, you try to reproduce what you see. But your body has its own habits, so familiar as to be unconscious. You are not aware that you carry your left shoulder higher than the right; to you they feel level. Your teacher, however, sees the discrepancy and brings it repeatedly to your attention until you learn to discern it for yourself and correct the imbalance that you now know to be there. You have begun to embody a specific teaching. You learn to rely on your heightened internal sense and not the correction of the external teacher. You have, you might say, begun to heal the imbalance that expressed itself in uneven shoulders. You come to feel, in a completely non-cognitive way, how the pose, the image of balance, expresses itself in you.

The asanas I have selected for this book are loosely organized around the central figure of Shiva, Lord of Yogis. Tradition says that Shiva created yoga at his wife Parvati's request, to help human beings free themselves from suffering.

Some asanas resonate directly with stories about Shiva and Parvati, others more to symbols, images, and attributes associated with India's sacred traditions. I think you will find a common theme of dealing with a puzzle or problem of human existence: suffering. The stories, characters, and images can affect us and transform us spiritually and emotionally, as the asanas affect us physically.

Approach these stories repeatedly, devotedly. Through listening to the stories and thinking about them; through looking at the artistic representations of Shiva, Parvati, and their attributes; through performing the asanas in a contemplative spirit; and finally through the self-examination process of journaling, we discover both who we are at this moment—or rather, who we think we are—and the possibility of moving beyond that. Through dwelling on them, we begin to incorporate some of the divine attributes that we contemplate. We rise to a new level of freedom and integrity in our asana practice and find greater richness and meaning in our lives off the mat.

Use this book in your personal practice, choosing a story, an asana, or an image to work with for the day, the weekend, or the week. Read the story. Practice the pose. Contemplate the image. Let them sink in and become part of you.

You may choose to journal about the process. Write about the sensation in your hip, your breath, something the story brought up, something that seems to have nothing to do with this pose but that wants to come out. It's about seeing what is present in your consciousness, not about creating a finished piece for publication. Choose a limit for each piece of writing—three pages, or fifteen minutes—stopping only when you reach that limit.

We all know the yoga maxim "As on the mat, so in life." If we are persistent, our asana practice can reveal not only which joints or muscles are in need of strengthening or realignment but also where we are impatient, lazy, unkind; and, let's hope, also where we are patient, dedicated, forgiving. The stories in this book offer opportunities to consider yourself against the background of stories that hold meaning for all people, for all time, and to "true your standard" against eternal values.

When I was a child, I heard my guru tell stories about Shiva, Rama, Krishna, and their wives, friends, and challenges. He would say that these stories and these people are alive right now, in us. As an adult I continue to derive tremendous joy and inspiration from yoga and from the art and mythology of India's sacred culture. The more I learn, the more I am surprised and delighted by new facets of the jewel that is yoga. I hope that my enthusiasm will be contagious and that you will find things in this book to surprise and delight you.

Introduction
A Personal Journey

The idea for this book was born at a week-long Relax and Renew teacher training held by Judith Lasater in Edmonton, Alberta. We were sharing observations of the way emotions have of coming up for various people in various poses, and how we as teachers could best respond when one student is obviously feeling something very deeply—sobbing, say—while all other members of the class serenely go on with their practice.

One woman shared a story about being in a class where a man who was practicing a pose on the next mat seemed ready to explode with fury. His face got red, his breathing was labored, he looked (she thought) as if he'd like to murder someone; and she was, well, a tad uneasy at being in such close proximity to his rage. Nothing bad happened, but she hadn't been satisfied with the teacher's handling of the situation, and it was still on her mind. "What pose were you doing?" someone asked. "*Virabhadrasana*—warrior 2."

"Wow!" I said, "Do you know who Virabhadra is?" Nobody did, or at least nobody else wanted to get up and share with the class. I told the story of Shiva's wedding, Daksha's sacrifice, and how the embodiment of rage and grief had been created from one of Shiva's hairs. We all marveled at the coincidence, if you want to call it that, of this pose being the one in which her fellow student was overcome with rage. Later, someone asked me to recommend a book telling the stories behind the yoga poses. I couldn't think of a single title. After a second I realized there was no such book, and the idea for this book was born. There are plenty of sources for tales from Indian mythology, and some modern yoga classics, such as the works of B. K. S. Iyengar, incorporate a few stories in discussions of the asanas. But you pretty much have to run across them by accident or else know what story you're looking for in order to find it.

The yoga tradition is very rich and very old. It's also very Indian, and this poses something of a problem, or a challenge, to modern American students.

I was introduced to yoga in 1964 when I was fourteen. That was the summer after President Kennedy was killed, the summer of the Freedom Riders who traveled to the American South in their effort to end segregation against African Americans. Timothy Leary had been kicked out of Harvard, but LSD was so uncommon that it wasn't yet illegal. The Beatles had not yet met the Maharishi. The war in Vietnam was barely mentioned. Ladies wore gloves and stockings with seams up the back. Personal cassette players were a thing of the future; transistor radios were state of the art.

At my house, my grandmother had died, and my mother and I were engaged in mortal combat. She and I could not be under the same roof for too long without one of us (well, me) running into her room yelling, "I hate you!" and slamming the door. My father spent a lot of time off somewhere, working, and my brother was temporarily lost to me in a world of sports. I was too young to have a job, too young to do *anything*, I thought, and anyway I had no transportation. I did what many a teenage girl has done in similar circumstances: I declared myself an atheist, wrote poetry, and thought about death.

They say that when the student is ready, the teacher appears. Mine appeared in the form of Dr. Rammurti S. Mishra and the community of the Ananda Ashram. Dr. Mishra was from India. He came from a family of meditators and Sanskritists, and he was then on staff at Bellevue, Manhattan's foremost public psychiatric hospital. He had developed a reputation in the medical community for being able to make progress with difficult, even hopeless-seeming, patients by the then-unheard-of measure of teaching them to meditate. One of his students acquired an old estate near Harriman, New York, and in the summer of 1964 it was getting ready to open its doors as an ashram, a place where people could come to study meditation, Sanskrit, and yoga. Dr. Mishra's book *Fundamentals of Yoga* had received some attention, and his lectures were popular in the city. He would work all week at Bellevue and travel to Harriman on weekends; meanwhile, a small core of his serious students and some ambiguous people with no visible means of support would stay on the property to develop it.

My parents were interested. They were Quakers and familiar with meditation. Krishnamurti and Mahatma Gandhi were two of my father's heroes. My parents attended a couple of meditation programs at Ananda but found themselves defeated by the length of the programs and the impenetrability of Dr. Mishra's accent. "I couldn't understand a word he said!" my mother complained later. However, they met a nice young man who was living there, who wanted to make some money giving guitar lessons. Just the thing for their sulky daughter! I did learn to play a few chords from Max, and before long my relieved mother was dropping me off at the ashram in the morning and picking me up in time for supper. My hanging around all day was justified by the semi-fiction that I was helping look after the younger children of a few of the residents.

I no longer recall any particular moment of meeting Dr. Mishra. I do recall his telling me that *ashram* meant a "refuge," and *ananda* meant "joy"—joyous refuge—and the ashram was that for me. I took to meditation as though to my natural element, and to the sporadic yoga classes with glee. I was a flexible kid, and Doctorji's method of teaching asana to children was to show us a pose and say invitingly, "Can you do this?" I trusted him completely. If he suggested that I could do it, I felt that surely I could, so I was never afraid to try anything.

As he taught, he told stories about the poses and the ancient yogis who discovered them. He contended that we already knew everything we needed—all the poses were already present inside us, along with Sanskrit and the wisdom of the Veda. "Feel it!" he said over and over. "It is your true nature."

"But what if I don't feel it?"

"It is *maya!*" he said promptly. Maya was the principle of illusion that tricked us into believing we were something other than eternal, imperishable—the same as God. "Omnipotent, omnipresent, omniscient," he would intone, my first adjectives for Divinity. "Thou art that!"

Some of the older and more serious meditators viewed me as intrusive, and I can see now that I must have been. My mother would drop me off when it worked for her, and the ashram's schedule was flexible at best. Programs lasted for hours, a mix of Sanskrit chanting, lecture, and meditation; as often as not, I burst cheerfully into the middle of something and rushed over to hug Doctorji, whom I regarded as my particular friend. He always hugged back, then said, "Now go sit down," which I would do, beaming, stepping carefully through the seated meditators as they glared at me, or smiled back, depending on how they felt about children.

Fourteen is such a vulnerable age. More than anything in my life right then, I needed an adult to tell me that in my inmost, realest nature I was valuable, eternal, already possessed of all the wisdom of the ages. I needed a tool to help me deal with my mother's sorrow, my father's absences, my feeling of being from another planet—and meditation gave me that. As I understood it, sitting in meditation and moving in meditation—asana—were just different aspects of the same process. "Like matter," said Doctorji, "sometimes a point, sometimes a wave." He also taught us to chant, the feel of the Sanskrit syllables rolling in the mouth and throat like grapes: *om nama shivaya*, or just *Om*. "It is all you will ever need," he instructed. "*Om* contains the vibrations of all consciousness. *Om* will protect your mind. *Om* is God Himself."

Not long afterwards, I needed all those tools and more. I was molested by an adult I trusted, someone connected with the ashram—not Doctorji. Afraid

I'd lose my joyous refuge and get Doctorji in trouble if I told, I said nothing to anyone; but I was deeply, horribly traumatized. The man was sent away soon afterwards, following a violent confrontation with another resident. About what? I never knew. But that was the beginning of a long time of depression, confusion, and self-destructive behavior for me. Doctorji could see that something was very wrong, and he saw the tension that shimmered between me and my mother. I don't know what he said to her, but she stopped taking me to the ashram and began making snide comments about him. School started.

Eventually—by now I was fifteen—my mother decided the solution to my moodiness was to have me institutionalized, and she found a psychiatrist willing to commit me. There was very little understanding in those days about post-traumatic stress, or awareness of symptoms of sexual abuse; I was diagnosed with schizoaffective disorder. It was a fashionable diagnosis for adolescents at the time, just as it was fashionable to send your "problem child" to a mental hospital. The doctors at the nice private hospital in Westchester said I was so sick I might never function normally. I would undoubtedly be on heavy medication for years and years, probably life, and frequent office visits would be necessary to monitor me. Years later, I told this story to a mental health professional. His response was, "Did your parents have good insurance?" They had great insurance.

Desperate, I called Doctorji. He was a psychiatrist; could he not intervene? To his eternal credit, he did try. He met with my mother privately ("Go meditate," he said reassuringly as he closed the door), then with me, to say good-bye.

We sat together in his little room, and he told me to look at his forehead. "Don't think, don't blink." He chanted and guided me through a meditation. It seems to me now that he was planting some sort of spiritual depth charge in my heart, with timers set at intervals for the rest of my life. I was still terrified, but along with the terror there was a deep sense of peace and confidence. In the timeless place that really mattered, I was all right, and would be all right.

My mother took me away and left me in a mental hospital, where I had more than one hundred shock treatments, both electroconvulsive and insulin. Later, I learned that Doctorji had offered an alternative of daily meditation with him, but my mother had refused.

I did not see Doctorji for twenty-five years. By the time I did, he had had a devastating stroke, but he remembered me at once. Delighted, he turned to his assembled students. "She was with me at beginning! She was meditating when she was . . ." he held his hand low to the floor at the level of a small child's head.

Later, without preamble, he said, "I could do nothing. You were minor. If you had been major I might have done. But your mother . . ." He shook his head.

Later I learned that a lot of wild things had gone on in the 1960s at Ananda, and Doctor Mishra had been the object of various allegations. I missed all that. To me, he was a loving, nurturing adult friend when I was a child who desperately needed one, and the only person in my world to take a stand against packing a fifteen-year-old off for electroconvulsive therapy. He also gave me, in advance, the antidote that would prevent me from being destroyed by the psychiatrists' treatment: yoga. He got to me first with the assurance that in my true nature I was eternal, imperishable, beyond body and mind, infinite consciousness, infinite joy, and that I would come to realize this by meditating as much as possible. In the hospital, through the terrifying fog of shock treatment, I repeated my mantra as much as I could, and I held on for dear life to the assurance that there was something real, something eternal, something infinitely meaningful beyond what I was experiencing then—and that this was maya. I played Doctorji's voice in my head, the slow sonorous roll he used to lead guided meditations, "Deeply relax your body . . . feel the flow of electricity from your body to the stars . . ." I read my paperback *Bhagavad Gita*, which the hospital allowed me to keep, and I pretended I was a yogi preserving equanimity in all circumstances. Eventually, I was released.

I have not often told this story because it's so very personal—and so painful. But it explains my lifelong devotion to the yoga tradition: it saved my life. Without the grounding I had received at Ananda Ashram, I am not at all sure I would have survived four months in an asylum at that age. I have been a mental health counselor myself, as an adult, and the few people I have met who had that many shock treatments back in the 1960s are now permanently under case management. I was very, very fortunate. Most of us, thankfully, don't have to put our practice to that particular test, but we all have our own life crises and challenges. Your yoga practice can be a real friend and ally.

As for the man who was in a rage at the beginning of this story, I don't know what happened to him, but I hope he finds a teacher who will tell him the story of Virabhadra and teach him to meditate on it.

This book is written with gratitude to all of my teachers, but most especially to Rammurti S. Mishra and Judith Hanson Lasater.

Namaste.

Ganesha is Shiva and Parvati's first son.
Here they are at home at Mount Kailash,
with Nandi, the bull, at their feet.

Shiva, Parvati, and Yoga

Before me as I write is a modern Indian print of a longhaired man, wearing a tiger skin, with snakes draped around his neck like a garland and the crescent moon, like a pair of horns, in his hair; he sits cross-legged, while a bull peers benignly over his shoulder. His arm rests casually on a crutch, or a T-shaped staff. All over India, on calendars, postcards, matchbooks, on walls, on shawls, on buses, on movie posters, in temples, in caves, in every conceivable medium, his familiar image appears. This is Shiva, the Lord of Yogis, in his most beloved and popular pose. Nearly as popular are images of Shiva with his wife Parvati snuggled close or sitting beside him with their infant son Ganesh on her lap, for all the world as if the three of them had gone to have their picture taken for Christmas cards. Only they are in front of a cave, or sitting on a wild animal's back, or under a tree. And the baby has the head of an elephant. Natural as they look, this is not your average family. Or is it?

Parvati convinced Shiva to invent yoga out of compassion. Life is hard. Happiness is often elusive. We get sick, grow old, and die. We fall prey to the illusion that this is all there is. Understanding how hard it can be to maintain perspective, Parvati asked Shiva to invent a system that would help people to deal with the inevitable suffering that comes with life as a human, and he did. Therefore, he is honored as the first yoga teacher, and she as the first student. As the universal teacher Dakshinamurti, he sits on Mount Kailash at the northernmost point of India, facing south (*dakshina* in Sanskrit) looking down on the entire world, one hand lifted in the gesture that means, "Fear not."

Shiva is known as the destroyer in the Indian trinity of Brahma (creator), Vishnu (preserver), and Shiva; but what he destroys is negativity, illusion, the things that have to go in order to make room for new creation and a higher level of consciousness. The notion of Shiva destroying and re-creating the world in eternally repeating cycles reappears in twentieth-century cosmology with Einstein's theory of relativity, and with the discovery that our bodies are continually destroying and renewing their own cells—we are completely transformed every seven years.

In America, for all the current marketplace buzz, and the horrid hybrids of "Yogilates" and "Yogaerobics," many people still regard yoga as a bit esoteric, pursued by wild-eyed longhaired men in tiny loincloths who can wrap their feet around their necks. That, or a kind of aerobics for weaklings.

In India, where yoga has flourished in one form or another for centuries, it is both more and far less mainstream. The image of the cross-legged, longhaired figure we know as Shiva—the name means "auspicious"—is at least five thousand years old; seals from an ancient city in what is now Punjab show a man with horns, or possibly a crescent moon, on his head, sitting cross-legged surrounded by animals. The *Rig Veda* (1500–900 BCE), speaks of Rudra (the Howler), a wild archer whose arrows brought disease, but who also knew the properties of healing herbs. By around 900 BCE, Rudra had evolved into Shiva, an ascetic who lives by choice in dangerous, inhospitable places such as high, cold mountains; crossroads; or cemeteries. He sits on a tiger skin in the Himalayan Mountains, meditating; and through his meditation the world is maintained. His throat is blue, scarred by the deadly poison he once drank to save the world. His hair is long, matted, and in it live the moon and the river Ganga. His body is covered with ash. But although he is eternally in meditation, the Lord of Ascetics is a family man, with a beautiful wife, children, animals to care for—not to mention the entire universe—and an infinite range of responsibilities.

Shiva is said to have invented eighty-four basic asanas to help people purify their bodies and prepare them for meditation. That kind of yoga is called *hatha yoga*, meaning a yoga involving forcefulness, determination. I heard yoga instructor Ramanand Patel explain hatha this way: "Think of a four-year-old who is determined not to let you pick him up. You do pick him up, and he makes his body rigid, he yells, he struggles, he will *not* stop fighting you even though you are much bigger and stronger and there is no way he actually can win, but he does not give up." That, said Ramanand, is the quality of hatha. That quality, applied to physical discipline, prepares you for the mental and spiritual discipline of meditation, *raja* (royal) yoga.

If you have a yoga practice, you will have noticed that it involves your whole being. You can't surgically remove the mind from the body, and what you do with your body affects your mind, your emotions, your neurons, and your body chemistry. But nobody says, "Ah, I have successfully reduced the acidity of my blood gases!" after a satisfying practice; instead they say, "Wow, I feel great!" You can only be aware of what you experience, and most of us start off with unrefined awareness. But what you do on your mat carries over into your life, and conversely. Your practice is like a mirror of your life. Are you straining and forcing your way through your practice? You're probably doing that in some other areas. Can you figure out through your practice how to be a little more compassionate with your own shortcomings, with your tight hamstrings, with your spouse's annoying way of expecting you to know where the widgets are? Do you find it hard to find *time* to practice? Ha! Could you possibly be neglecting your health or spiritual well-being in any other ways?

Yoga is ultimately about relationship: the relationship of spirit and matter, body and soul, intention and action, teacher and student. You are both teacher and student, in relation to yourself as well as to others.

Go through every detail of your life and character and ask yourself, if this changed, or was gone, would I still be me? You know you would.

We can't really name it, but we know it. There is an essence you share with every person on the planet. When we say *namaste* at the end of class, we invoke that unity. Its pursuit is why we study yoga. And that essence, that ground of being—that is Shiva.

Shiva personifies the One, the cosmic human being with infinite forms but one essence. In the stories we see him as a lover, a bereaved husband, a warrior, a family man, a teacher, an intercessor for the community, the unmoving contemplative in the mountains, and the eternally moving dancer in the flames. He is free to engage in everything without being bound by anything. That freedom from bondage is the fruit of yoga.

When I was young, my teacher Sri Rammurti told stories about Shiva and other heroes from the Indian epics. He explained that all the characters in the stories were aspects of our own minds, making the stories instructive as well as entertaining. We can learn something about ourselves, or certain modes of behavior, from these stories. If the story is about a demon abducting a princess, there is a level on which we can enjoy the demon as a demon and the princess as a princess, but they are also psychological principles. The demon might represent ego, or selfishness, and the princess the mind or the soul. Even if we don't have an analytical grasp of the story's "meaning," we can still respond powerfully to its message. The Swiss psychologist Carl Jung suggested that each of us, consciously or unconsciously, has a myth that guides our life. Do you always seem to be charging in to rescue damsels in distress? Are you like the youngest son or daughter who has no inheritance and must live by his or her wits?

For this book, I have chosen stories about Shiva that illustrate or relate to various well-known asanas in the hope that your yoga practice will be enriched and enlivened by the presence of the story in your consciousness when you take to the mat. I believe that the postures themselves embody some of the energy of the stories, and I hope that knowing the story will help you to find the pose that emerges uniquely from your body and your experience—your story. Above all, I hope that you will enjoy these stories as much as I have.

Shiva arrives at his wedding wearing a tiger skin and with a retinue of goblins. As Sati greets him, her mother faints.

Shiva as Destroyer
Warrior Poses

Parvati was not Shiva's first wife. Shiva's first wife was Sati, the daughter of King Daksha. Daksha's job, since the beginning of the world, was to oversee and regulate rituals and see that they were done properly. Ancient beliefs hold that an improperly conducted ritual can adversely affect the kingdom, while one done according to correct procedure benefits everyone. If you plan to invoke divine powers, you had better know how to do it right.

Sati's parents did not see Shiva until the day of the wedding; they had to take their daughter's word that he was the love of her life and the Lord of the Universe (Jagadisha). At an Indian wedding, the groom comes to the bride's house on horseback, accompanied by all his friends. Shiva arrived in his aspect of the lord of burial grounds with long matted hair, his body covered in ashes, wreathed in snakes, and accompanied by a troop of ghosts and demons all reeking of *bhang* (a marijuana derivative). Sati knew him well enough not to be deceived by appearances, but her poor parents were appalled and wanted to cancel the wedding. Finally, to please Sati, Shiva showed himself in his magnificent aspect, radiantly handsome, garlanded with gold, dressed in silk, and accompanied by splendid, deferential courtiers. That's more like it, thought Daksha, and allowed the marriage to proceed; but he held a grudge.

A short time later, Daksha sent invitations to everyone he knew and a few he didn't know to attend a splendid *yagya* at his court. A yagya is a religious ceremony, a sacrifice involving fire; it can go on for several days, and a king's yagya is a very special occasion indeed. No invitation came for Sati and Shiva.

"Surely," said Sati with a sinking heart, "he just forgot. Of course he means us to be there."

Shiva was not so sure; or rather, he was quite sure, but tried not to upset his wife. "Your father doesn't like me," he said, "and he knows where we live. If he wanted us there he'd have said so. You go if you want, but I am not going to make matters worse by crashing his party."

"I will," said Sati, and set off with her women for her father's house.

It was clear that she was not welcome. Daksha and his friends said insulting things about her husband, her wedding, her taste in men— and their remarks got worse as the evening wore on. The yagya was a mockery of itself, with the Lord of the Universe excluded and insulted. Daksha was offering nothing of real value; he was simply flaunting his own wealth and power. That One to whom all sacrifice ultimately comes was not present. The Veda tells us that in a true sacrifice, God is the offering, the one who offers, the recipient, the flames, the fuel, the ritual. This was no sacrifice! Sati could not bear it. The flames roared. With one swift movement she flung herself into the fire and was burned to ash, herself becoming the sacrifice.

When Shiva heard what had happened, he was overcome with grief and fury. His eyes stood out, his blood boiled, his hair stood on end. In an ecstasy of rage, he tore a hair from his own head and flung it to the ground. The next moment, where the hair had been stood a warrior, the personification of Shiva's emotions, red-faced and grunting with the lust for vengeance. This was Virabhadra, the personification of righteous anger and the noble impulse to defend the innocent.

The warrior Virabhadra saluted Shiva, then flew to King Daksha's palace where he ripped and roared through the sacrifice, destroying everyone and everything in his path. He tore off Daksha's head. There is more to the story of his depredations, but this is not the place to tell it. As for Sati, she was reborn as Parvati, this time with a father who supported Shiva and her love for him. As for Daksha, Shiva forgave him and restored him to life, but he had to live with the head of a goat.

In the three poses named for Virabhadra, we see a progression from the warrior offering his efforts to his higher power, to one moving dynamically but with control into action.

Warrior Poses *(virabhadrasana)*

Embodying the Pose

Warrior 2

Stand with the inner edges of your feet just touching. Inhaling, step the feet as wide as one of your legs is long, and open the arms wide. Exhaling, turn your right heel in and your left leg out. Rotate the muscles of both thighs from the midline of the body to the outside edges. Keep the arms wide, palms down, at shoulder height. Exhaling, bend your left knee, drop the top of the thighbone, lift the left hipbone. Exhaling, turn the head to look over your front arm.

Warrior 1

Inhaling, rotate your arms from the shoulder blades and lift them overhead; join the palms. Inhaling, step the legs wide. Exhaling, turn the right heel in, and bring your pelvis around to face the left leg. Exhaling, bend the left knee, tracking it over your second and third toes. Lift the spine and the chest even more. Draw the shoulder blades forward to open the chest and collarbones. Lift the base of the skull.

Distribute your weight evenly between the front foot and back foot. Widen the shoulder blades. Lift the heart. Feel the strength and stability of your arms and legs.

Warrior 3

From warrior 1, exhale and lower the arms till they are parallel with the floor. Unclasp the hands; extend the arms from the shoulder blades through the tips of the little fingers. Exhaling, straighten the front knee and simultaneously lift the back leg, keeping the hips level, until the thigh is parallel with the floor. Feel how the backward thrust of the leg balances the forward reaching of the arms.

Sustaining the Pose

In each of these poses, notice the dynamic play between your body and your breath. They are traditionally known as 1, 2, and 3 not because of sequence, but because there are that many limbs extended. How does the joining or releasing of the hands affect your breathing? Your sense of strength? Where do you feel most solid, most stable? What thoughts or feelings arise in you as you hold each pose?

Releasing the Pose

Exhaling, lower your arms and return to standing.

Points for Practice

What are the physical symptoms of anger in you? Of grief?

Sit in any comfortable neutral position. Notice the placement and quality of your breath, the quality of your eyes and hands.

Harden and thrust out your lower jaw. Flare your nostrils. Did your head come forward as you did this? Did you tighten the base of your skull? Did the hands or fingers harden? Let your eyes stare and become hard. Notice your breathing. Notice how you feel emotionally. Are sensations of anger beginning to arise?

Now drop your head, round your shoulders, collapse your chest. Cup your forehead in your hands. Open the back of the throat, exhale from the belly as if you were sobbing silently. What emotions begin to arise?

Come to a neutral seated position with the spine erect, supported if you like, as long as your head is free to move. Support the forearms and hands on your lap, palms up; if there is the faintest sense of dragging in the shoulders or hardness in the hands, support the hands and forearms on a folded blanket or cushion until the arms feel weightless. Balance the crown of the head over the tailbone and lift the breastbone naturally. Now lift the base of the skull so that the chin tilts downward slightly, and the eyes naturally turn downward. Observe your breathing; observe your mind. Observe what emotions arise.

Stand on both feet equally, the inner edges just touching, notic-ing your breath, your weight distribution, the position of your rib cage, the way your eyes feel in your head. How do you feel emotionally as you stand in a neutral position? Inhaling, step the feet wide and bring the arms to shoulder height, palms facing down. Did your breathing change? Exhaling, turn out your front leg, bend the knee, and come into warrior 2. Notice your breath, your eyes, your weight, your ribs. Is there a tendency to put more weight and more energy into the bent-knee side of the body? Does it seem more important that the straight-leg side? How does this pose feel physically? How does it feel emotionally? Is it difficult? Do you harden your eyes and breath in this or other "hard" poses? Can you shift awareness to the back leg, the back ribs, without sacrificing your sense of alertness? Are you just waiting to move out of this position into something else, something more comfortable, some-thing more challenging, more interesting, more important? Commit to spending five more breaths here. What does your mind do?

Standing on both feet equally, inhale and swing both arms overhead and join the hands. Notice how the front ribs tend to flare while the back ribs and the area behind the heart close. Notice your breathing. Does this stance feel aggressive?

Draw the rib cage toward the back body, widening the area between the shoulder blades. Notice how the breath changes. Does this change the emotional quality of the stance?

Can you experience sadness when the back of the heart is closed and the front ribs are flared? Do you use anger or aggression to protect yourself from feeling too sad?

Widen the feet, turn the hips, and come into warrior 1. Observe the ribs, the breath, the placement of your weight. Does everything in the pose move forward? Do you lose awareness of your back body? Does the breath change, perhaps becoming shorter and higher as if you were ready to fight or flee?

Shift the weight to the back heel, open the back ribs, invite the breath into the space behind your heart. Move the head behind your upraised arms; from the base of the skull, look up. Notice how chang-ing the angle and placement of the head affects the feeling of the pose. Do you have a sense of feeling more aggressive or more prayerful if you move your head forward or backward? Practice lifting the head from the chin, from the base of the skull, and from between the shoulder blades. How do these three ways feel different?

From warrior 1, slowly shift into warrior 3. Where is your center of balance? Do your back body and your lifted leg tend to fall into unconsciousness as you lift and come forward? What happens to the ribs? What happens to the breath and to the space between your shoulder blades? What is the quality in the eyes? Do they tend to stare and harden? Can you keep them soft without losing focus?

How easy is it to keep your heart open and calm when you move into action, especially into defensive action?

Journaling

Reflect and journal on a time when you came to the defense of a righteous cause or an innocent person. Invite the emotional qualities of that experience into your practice of the warrior poses. Keep the experience in mind while practicing with softness in the eyes and openness in the heart.

Where, for you, is the line between laziness and intelligent inaction? Where is the line between intelligent action and thoughtless rage?

*Ardhanarishvara combines opposites.
Shiva with Nandi on the left and the
Goddess with her lion on the right.*

Parvati
Mountain Pose

Shiva's wife Sati was dead, burnt in Daksha's *yagya*. Insane with grief, Shiva roamed all over India, carrying his dead wife's body, until the gods intervened. Vishnu sent his sharp-edged discus to cut up Sati's body, making pieces drop off, and forcing Shiva to relinquish it. Then Shiva went to his cave in the mountains to meditate.

After a long time, the goddess who had been Sati was reborn as Parvati, the daughter of Mount Himavat (also known as Himalaya) and the celestial nymph Menaka. Her name means "mountain," and places where two peaks come together are regarded as her breasts.

Determined to win Shiva's love, the Daughter of the Mountain adopted an asceticism to rival his own. She dressed in bark garments like a yogi, fasted extensively, stood motionless for hours in asanas to hone her concentration and master her body and mind. Her discipline *(tapas)* was so extraordinary that its energy inwardly communicated kinship to Shiva as he sat deep in meditation, and roused him from *samadhi*. In the form of a wandering mendicant accompanied by a dog, he intruded on Parvati's tapas and taunted her, casting aspersions on her resolve, her abilities and qualifications as a renunciate, and ultimately on her ideal, Shiva. Parvati preserved her equanimity as long as she was being insulted; but when it came to Shiva, she became passionate in his defense—so passionate that Shiva's reserve finally melted. Even as she spoke, he revealed himself through his disguise. When she recognized him, she fell silent, and the god and goddess were reunited.

Their perfect unity, the way they form complementary halves of one whole, is expressed visually in the form of Ardhanarishvara. The story goes that Shiva's devotee, Bhrigu, grew resentful of his lord's intimacy with Parvati and wanted to separate them. He desired to worship only Shiva by circumambulating his body, but Shiva embraced Parvati so closely that not even a tiny insect could come between them. To free Bhrigu from his jealousy, Shiva revealed himself as Ardhanarish-vara—the Lord who is Half Man, Half Woman, both Shiva and Parvati inseparably, the embodiment of non-duality.

Images of this form of Shiva show one half of his body with the rounded hip, full breast, and ornaments of a woman, while the other half has a flat muscular chest, the powerful thigh of a warrior, and a warrior's earring. Nevertheless the overall effect is one of harmony, if not symmetry.

Mountain Pose *(tadasana)*

Embodying the Pose

Also known as *samapada* or *samasthiti* (both indicating a balanced or equal stance), *tadasana* evokes stability and firmness. The *stha* element in Sanskrit, which survives in such English words as *standing, still, stable, stoic,* and *steady,* carries the sense of firmness, unmovingness, balance, equality. The two sides of the body, though not perfectly symmetrical, are held in balance, each side supporting the other with its strengths and being equally supported. The steady interplay of action and rest between the two sides gives the pose its dynamic quality. As taught today in most yoga classes, tadasana requires standing with feet either joined or parallel, the two sides of the body balanced along the midline of the spine, crown of the head balanced over the tailbone, and the arms at the sides.

Stand with your feet parallel to one another, either with the inner edges of the feet joined or with the feet hip-width apart. Hip-width means the hipbones: align the hipbones over the knees and the knees over the ankles, creating a firm foundation. Spread the toes, lift the inner arches of the feet. Notice where your weight falls—to the front or to the back of the foot, to the outer edge or the inner edge? Adjust minutely, till both feet feel equally broad and your weight is distributed evenly over the sole of each foot.

Coming up the body from the foundation, notice your hips. Are they level? Is the distance the same between your left hip and your bottommost left rib, and your right hip and your bottommost right rib? Is either side of the rib cage rotated more toward the front than the other side? Are your shoulders level? Adjust. Place your right arm along the midline of your right side, fingers pointing down. Place your left arm along the midline of your left side, fingers pointing down. Notice the shape of your shoulders between the neck and the top of the upper arm. If they drop like the sides of a hanger, and if this creates a sense of drag on the upper inner arms, gently lift the outer edges of the shoulders. Notice what effect this action has on your neck and head. Find the crown of the head and bring the center of the top of your skull in line with the tailbone.

Sustaining the Pose

Standing with your weight distributed equally between the two sides of your body, feet parallel, place your attention at your right nostril. Breathe in, keeping your attention on sensations in the right lung and the entire right side of the body. When that side is full, bring the attention to the midline of your body, cross it, and exhale through the left nostril. Then inhale on the left, and repeat the process for 15 minutes or until you are tired, noticing the qualities of your right side and your left side. Do you have a sense of one side being brighter, one darker; one stronger, one more flexible; one active, one more passive; one masculine, one feminine? Can you find the middle ground where the two sides come together and sustain one another?

Releasing the Pose

Exhaling, step forward. Which foot do you naturally move first? Relax.

Points for Practice

Our bodies are not symmetrical. We can achieve balance, but never symmetry. One lung is larger. Some people have different vision in each eye, possibly one eye or ear slightly higher than the other. We all have dominant hands and feet, not necessarily on the same side of the body. Injuries aside, our muscles rarely develop exactly the same on both sides. Our life histories are written in our bodies.

If you have ever had surgery, which side was it on? What about dental work? Injuries? Headaches? Have more things "happened" to one side than the other? Is it the one you consider stronger, or weaker? Make a written inventory of each side of your body's experiences and characteristics. As you move through the world this week, notice which hand you use more often, which foot you usually step forward with, which leg is on top if you cross your legs or ankles. Practice reversing that, and notice how you feel.

Do you think of yourself as having a "good" side, or find that you like some qualities of your body more than others? We often speak of having a "bad" knee when we mean it is weaker or has been injured. Notice the things about yourself and your body that you would like to push away, as Bhrigu wanted to remove Parvati so he could worship Shiva alone. Practice accepting all of yourself, particularly the parts that are harder to love.

Shiva sits for meditation on his tiger skin, with snakes, a trident, an ascetic's water pot, and Ganga flowing from his hair.

Shiva in Meditation

Easy Pose

Sthira-sukham asanam, the *Yoga Sutra* tells us, "Stability and ease are the defining qualities of asana." *Sukha,* the quality of being relaxed, comfortable, at ease, is often contrasted with its opposite, *dukha,* the quality of suffering, not being at ease.

The *Hatha Yoga Pradipika* by the yogi Swami Svatmarama opens with salutations to Shiva, the Lord of Yogis, who taught his wife Parvati hatha yoga as the first step to the pinnacle of raja yoga. In classifying the eight limbs of raja yoga in the *Yoga Sutra,* Patanjali lists the hatha yoga disciplines of *asana* and *pranayama* after the ethical principles (the *yamas* and *niyamas*) but before the four meditative limbs.

Notice the priority expressed in both texts: asana practice is not an end in itself. In a stable, comfortable posture, we create a physical environment that can nurture sustained meditation. Sukha is not only a matter of physical ease and comfort but also of intelligence and of the willingness to let go of preconceptions and stay with the process. Thus *sukhasana* is the basic seated posture for meditation, which is, after all, the real way and the goal of yoga practice.

As Yogishvara, the Lord of Yogis, Shiva sits in meditation in the mountains. While his two earthly eyes are closed, he keeps eternal watch over human beings with his "third eye," the sensitive intuitive center between his eyebrows. In this position he becomes so calm and stable that he has mastery over all his senses, represented by the snake coiled round his neck like a garland and the tiger skin he uses as a seat. In his hands he holds a trident, representing the threefold nature of the universe, and a small drum, which evokes the rhythm of time. The crescent moon rides in his hair as an emblem of time and change against the unchanging background of his easy, comfortable, eternal stance.

Easy Pose *(sukhasana)*

Embodying the Pose

Sit on the floor with your legs straight in front of you. Bend your left knee. Hold your left foot with your hands and draw the heel close to your right sit bone. Now bend the right knee and bring the right shin in front of the left shin, in a simple cross-legged position. Tuck your right foot under your left knee or thigh. Rest your hands in your lap. *Note: Your hip joints should be higher than your knees.* Use a cushion or a folded blanket to elevate the pelvis relative to the knee joint.

Pay attention to your knees! If you feel strain or pain in either knee, adjust the height of your seat, and try placing a folded blanket or a yoga block near the top of the thighbone. Place props near the hip rather than directly under the knee, and if you support one knee, support the other at the same height to preserve your body's sense of balance.

Do you need to sit on a folded blanket or a bolster to create enough space for your thighs to drop?

Do you need to support your knees by putting a folded blanket or a block or something under the tops of the thighbones?

Have you sickled the ankle on either foot? The ankles and knees are more flexible than the hips, but this pose calls for you to open your hips. Don't let those flexible lower joints trick you into letting them do the job instead.

If you experience a sense of drag or strain in the shoulders or arms, place a long folded blanket across your lap to support the forearms and wrists. Try placing an eyebag under each wrist. With the right placement of the hands and forearms, the shoulders will feel alert but relaxed.

This pose is recommended for meditation and seated pranayama. Be honest with yourself about how much support your body needs to be steady and comfortable for 20 minutes or more.

Sustaining the Pose

Once you have established a firm and honest base, draw the sacrum toward your front body and lift your spine. Slide the rib cage up as if your head, ribs, and pelvis were beads on the string of the spine, and you were holding the bottom bead down and pulling the string gently from the top. Sense the crown of the head balanced over the tailbone.

Rest the backs of your hands on your knees, palms up, thumbs and forefingers joined (like the "O.K." gesture), keeping the other fingers extended, not rigid. This gesture, known as a *mudra*, represents the individual consciousness or ego (the forefinger) joining itself to divine wisdom (the thumb). The three extended fingers represent the world of the three *gunas* (innate universal qualities). In other words, the hand gesture illustrates the commitment to live your life in accordance with what you perceive as truth, instead of letting your base desires run things. This, of course, is what meditation does: it provides an opportunity for our impulses to run their course harmlessly, without having to be made manifest, while we watch the action and keep returning our attention to the stable point we've chosen.

As you sit cross-legged with a broad base, imagine yourself taking the form of a mountain with your head as the peak, your sides and arms as the slopes, and your thighs and feet as the base. Send your awareness deep into the earth for the roots of this mountain.

What do you notice about your breathing as you settle into this pose? Does your mind offer any resistance to becoming physically still? Do you notice movement in your eyes? Does lowering and focusing your gaze affect the movement of the breath? Of the mind?

In Mammoth Cave, Kentucky, Native Americans noticed that air appeared to flow out of the cave in the winter and into the cave in the summer. They thought of this as the earth taking very slow breaths— inhaling in the warm half of the year, exhaling in the cold half. Small, quick things breathe quickly, so it makes sense that something as large as the earth might well only complete one cycle of breath in a year. How would a mountain breathe?

Imagine yourself as Shiva, the yogi sitting still on top of the mountain, solid and steady as the earth itself, but eternally alert. How is it for you to be relaxed and alert at the same time? Can you maintain a sense of alertness and sensitivity in the forehead while your two eyes are closed?

Releasing the Pose

Exhale, release your feet and stretch the legs. When you have relaxed for a bit, repeat for the same length of time with the other foot in front.

A south Indian depiction of Shiva with his attendants, dancing on the personification of Ignorance.

Shiva Dancing
King Dancer Pose

Shiva is not only the lord of stillness and contemplation, but the lord of all that lives and moves. The *Kena Upanishad* asks what it is by which the ear hears, the eyes see, the limbs move, and so on; you could say in answer to any of those questions, "Shiva." The eighth-century sage Shankaracharya, who is sometimes regarded as an incarnation of Shiva, wrote a beautiful poem in which the soul goes, step by step, through all the things it is not in the ultimate sense, each time concluding, "I am the form of bliss, I am Shiva, I am Shiva." Shiva thus identifies, or names, our most profound level of being. We can think of "reality" as something that changes constantly, takes one form and then another, always in process of transformation from one state to the next, even when the surface might appear to be still.

Look at an apple or a rock. Not much change will take place in the next hour, or even day, unless you intervene—drop it, or break it, or put it in water or fire. But the molecules are changing, some things are breaking down and others are forming. In the case of the apple, within a week, you will see it begin to rot, which is a way of changing form so that new apples can be born from the seeds of this one. In the case of the rock, change may not be visible in your lifetime. That principle that causes change—encompassing both the death and decay of the old apple and the sprouting seeds that will someday produce new apples—that principle is Shiva, Lord of the Dance.

In the Nataraja statues, Shiva dances alone in a ring of flame. When this image has four arms, one hand holds the drum, signifying both the rhythm of time and our own heartbeats; another gestures toward his lifted foot. A third hand is raised in *abhaya mudra,* which resembles our modern gesture for "stop," but in this case signifies "fear not." The fourth is in teaching mode. One foot, usually the left, is crushing a small misshapen figure representing ignorant action, while the other lifts, indicating liberation.

A particularly fierce form of his dance is the *tandava*—a stamping, powerful, high-energy style associated today with South Indian dance, rather resembling an Eastern form of the flamenco. Some people think the dance traveled from India to Spain in gypsy caravans. The story says that out of fury and rage Shiva created the warrior Virabhadra when his first wife, Sati, was killed, and danced in a frenzy of love and grief with her corpse in his arms until Vishnu cut it into pieces.

The pose of *natarajasana* requires strength, great flexibility, and great stability. It teaches us to remain balanced even in the middle of intense emotion and activity, and reminds us that all acts of destruction are followed by resurrection. It also challenges us to recognize our limits.

King Dancer Pose *(natarajasana)*

Embodying the Pose
Stand in *tadasana*. Exhaling, bend one knee and bring the foot up behind you. Reaching behind you with the arm on the same side, catch the foot or ankle with your hand or a strap.

Move your tailbone toward the floor. Drop the weight of the bent leg from your pelvis, drawing the foot toward your head, stretching the front thigh.

Inhale and extend the free arm from the shoulder.

Exhale, still holding the foot, and bring your torso parallel with the floor, extending one arm in front, holding the lifted foot with the other hand.

Alternatives

- Reach overhead with one arm, extending the front arm. Hold the lifted foot with the back hand, forming a bow shape on that side of the body.
- Reach overhead with both arms, and clasp the lifted foot with both hands. Draw the shoulder blades forward, bringing the upper chest into a backbend, balancing the forward movement of the chest with the upward impetus of the back foot.
- Practice with your back facing a wall; when you lift the back leg, rest the shin on the wall for balance.

The torso in these versions remains upright.

Sustaining the Pose

Keep the soles of your feet intelligent; feel your base. Let the upward movement of the pose be grounded in the firmness of the standing leg and foot. Where do you experience lines of energy balancing one another? How is your breathing? What is your facial expression? Does your pose feel more like a dance of grief and anger, holding it together in the face of great tragedy and stress, or more like a playful dance of exploring your limits? Where do you notice your breath most clearly in this pose?

Releasing the Pose

Come out elegantly. Exhaling, release the grip on the foot and lower it to the floor. Bring the arms to the sides. Stand easily in tadasana.

Points for Practice

This is a challenging pose, and the full pose may not be readily accessible to all students. It is rarely included in "how-to" yoga books for the good reason that it is best learned under the personal supervision of an experienced teacher. It resembles the bow pose in the action of the arms, shoulders, and back, and it resembles warrior 3 in being a standing balancing pose in which one arm is sometimes extended to the front while the weight is balanced by a backward movement of the lifted leg.

How far are you willing to go to challenge yourself? Do you approach some asanas as win/lose competitions? Are you apt to criticize yourself for not doing difficult things easily? What is ignorant action? What is intelligent action? What is ignorant inaction? What is intelligent inaction?

Lord Dattatreya embodies Brahma, Vishnu, and Shiva in one body with three faces. The four dogs represent the four Vedas.

The Three Faces of Dattatreya
Triangle Pose

The universe is triform in nature, the sages tell us, and there are trinities everywhere we look. The creation, preservation, and destruction of the world is looked over by Brahma, Vishnu, and Shiva; our individual existence is governed by the inescapable triad of birth, life, and death. The three constitutions of Ayurveda are drawn from the even more basic concept of three *gunas*, three "strands" which constitute the "fabric" of physical being; and the body has three main energy channels *(ida, pingala,* and *sushumna).*

In the Nath tradition of western India, Lord Dattatreya is regarded as an incarnation of Shiva. Like Shiva, he is a wandering renunciate, and as Shiva is the First Teacher of all yogis, Dattatreya is the First Teacher of that particular yoga tradition. Like Shiva in his Bhairava form, Dattatreya is generally accompanied by dogs—in his case, four dogs that represent the Vedas.

Dattatreya is a mysterious figure, half-historical, half-mythological, who is depicted in Indian iconography with three faces, representing Brahma, Vishnu, and Shiva. He sits with his begging bowl near the wish-fulfilling cow, surrounded by his dogs, with a *dhuni* (fire-pit) in front of him. While the three tines of Shiva's trident represent the body's three main energy channels, Dattatreya's trident indicates transcendence of the three gunas through renunciation. Artistic representations of Datta-treya are filled with subtle triads and triangular shapes such as the almost flame-like shape of his hair or the bends of his elbow and crossed leg.

Dattatreya collects ignorance, attachment, aversion, and clinging to life from his followers (the qualities which cause our suffering and our sense of being bound to the world) and throws them to his dogs to eat as treats. Our sense of personal ego, he throws into his dhuni to be consumed by the fire of *tapas* (persistent effort) and divine love. In your practice, imagine offering your personal limitations into the flame of your body's tapas.

All yoga poses unfold in three phases. Embodying the pose (evolu-tion: the pose coming out of your body) flows into sustaining the pose (duration: the subtle changes that occur as you remain in this position for a length of time). Releasing the pose (involution: letting go of the shape you have assumed, and returning your body to its original state) follows naturally when the activity is complete.

Triangle Pose *(trikonasana)*

Embodying the Pose
Begin in *tadasana*. Exhaling, step or jump the feet wide apart, about as wide as one of your legs is long. You are creating the base of the triangle. Exhaling, externally rotate your left leg ninety degrees from the hip. Rotate your right leg slightly in. Bring the arms to shoulder height. On the exhalation, keeping your right heel firmly on the floor, extend the ribs over the left leg, and bring the hand to the floor, or to your ankle, or to a block. Widen the shoulder blades and reach the right fingertips toward the ceiling.

Sustaining the Pose
Find the tailbone and the crown of the head, and see if they are in alignment. Lengthen the spine. A second triangle is formed by your

front leg, your front arm, and your spine, with your head at its apex. Notice your bottom ribs. Notice your top ribs. Are they parallel to one another? If the bottom ribs curve upward, elongate the spine and bring the bottom ribs closer to being parallel with the floor. Slide the shoulder blades down the back, drawing the shoulders away from the ears. At the same time, draw the lower flat edge of the shoulder blades toward the front body to support the opening and widening of the chest. Notice the triangular shapes of the shoulder blades and of the sternum. Lean back into your back body. Feel the relationship of your top arm to the armpit and upper ribs. There is a third triangle formed by this arm and the spine, whose third side is space. How well can you sense that shape? Can you imagine the points on your body where the third side meets your skin? Are you aware of other triangles in your body—sacrum, sternum, shoulder blades?

Notice how at every moment your breath comes into being, lasts for some duration, and then dissolves. Notice how the pose is supported by the breath as well as the muscles and bones; notice how the pose comes into being, is sustained—by what?—and changes with each breath even while it remains stable on the macro-level of bone and flesh. Notice your pelvis in relation to the legs, and how the legs are working differently in the hips.

Releasing the Pose

To return to tadasana, inhale and lift the top arm and ribs till the spine is vertical. Exhaling, bring both legs to a neutral forward-facing position and lower the arms to the sides.

Points for Practice

Triangle pose teaches us the great stability to be found in threeness. The limbs are asymmetrical, but the overall shape of the body allows you to achieve tremendous, dynamic balance. In this pose, explore not only the triangular shapes described by your limbs but also the inner experiences of forward action, backward action, ascending energy, descending energy, and stasis. All three qualities are present. Is one more present for you than the others? Always?

Imagine your body and mind as the formless medium of rock out of which the pose takes form; you are the medium, and you are also the sculptor who takes away everything that is not the pose. B. K. S. Iyengar suggests all that is not the pose is the individual ego. What do you need to lose or let go of in order for the pose to shine through?

Journaling

Journal about the phases you can discern in your life, in your day, in your practice. Look around you for triangles, or trinities, in nature, in the environment, in society. Does this shape appeal to you? Why or why not?

The Gunas

In Hindu cosmology, all consciousness and, indeed, all life, emanates from a single cosmic substance *(prakriti)*, which consists of three essential modes or qualities, the *gunas.* These are: *sattva,* the quality of illumination, purity, goodness, which produces clarity and serenity; *rajas,* the quality of activity or mobility, which makes a person not only active and energetic but also willful and tense; and *tamas,* the quality of darkness, stability, and restraint, which not only grounds but also obstructs the tendencies of rajas to move forward and of sattva to reveal. All three gunas are present everywhere at all times, but each of us is born with a certain mix that determines our primary tendencies. In folk art and pottery, the gunas are evoked by the colors red, white, and black.

Shiva's symbolic representation as a lingam, surrounded by offerings and protected by one of his cobras.

The Lord of Snakes
Cobra Pose

Shiva is often shown garlanded with snakes; this was one of the many things that Sati's parents objected to in their prospective son-in-law—along with his matted hair and troop of ghouls.

Snakes, especially cobras, have an honored place in Indian mythology. According to one story, the world itself is supported on the coils of the great serpent Ananta (the Endless). It is interesting that Norse mythology has the same image, only there the serpent is transformed into its cousin, the dragon. Serpents are mysterious: they shed their skins; cobras especially can live to be extremely old, making them symbols of rebirth and regeneration as well as ancient wisdom. As we all know, however, snakes can be dangerous. They may bite, they may strike, they may spit poison, they may crush smaller creatures to death in their embrace or swallow them whole. Snakes can go in a flash from stillness to unbelievably rapid movement, giving them a reputation for lying quietly in wait and then suddenly attacking.

On the other hand, snakes are known to enjoy music, and even to dance—not only to the snake charmer's flute but also alone. A lady I know once spent a few days in a bungalow in India, long ago, where one of the downstairs bedrooms could not be used because after dark it would fill with snakes who came in and danced. Footless but swift, wise but unpredictable, snakes seem to exist at some strange twist on the evolutionary chain: we humans can relate to them, or so it seems, but can you ever really know where you stand with a snake?

Patanjali, compiler of the *Yoga Sutra,* is sometimes said to be either an incarnation of the cosmic serpent Ananta, reborn at his own request so he could see Shiva dance again; or he is said to have been half-Naga. His statues show a figure whose lower half is made up of a serpent's coils, with the top half being human. The Snake People (Nagas) of mythology live underground where they guard buried treasure, like dragons in European traditions. There is an annual festival, Nag Panchami, in the month of July or August, when thousands of cobras are caught and brought to Shiva temples to be fed milk and honored with flowers. After a day of people snake-dancing in the streets, watching the snake-charmers' art, and displaying toy snakes for those who have no live ones of their own, the cobras are released unharmed. However, the Nagas are also a real tribe of forest dwellers and hunters who are among the oldest of India's aboriginal peoples. It is possible that the tradition saying Patanjali was half-Naga means that one of his parents was a member of this tribe. It may also be a way of saying that his work on yoga is a repository of ancient treasures of wisdom, wrought into a form human beings can use, just as the Nagas are the guardians of treasures and secrets.

Sometimes the energy in our spinal column is imaged as a snake, coiled at the tailbone, waiting to rise through various energy centers to the center of the brain. According to some schools of philosophy, when the energy potential centered in the lower body is awakened through yoga and meditation, that energy winds its way up the spinal column like a snake until it reaches the crown of the head, the highest energy center. At this point, it becomes conscious, and the meditator is enlightened. This is why so many statues of the Buddha, the very embodiment of enlightenment, show him with a cobra's hood flaring out around his head. Like the Buddha, Shiva has so mastered the mind, energy, and emotions that he is in no danger from a snake; he has the power, determination, and purity to neutralize all poisons, and to him the snake becomes a garland or an ornament.

Cobra Pose *(bhujangasana)*

Embodying the Pose

Lie on the floor, face down. Extend the legs, keeping the feet together, tops of the feet on the floor. Keep the knees straight, legs active, toenails pressing down. Draw the tailbone toward the pubis. Bring the hands, palms down, to the floor along your waist. Inhaling, press the palms into the floor and lift the torso. Inhaling, lift the spine and chest still more; keep drawing the tailbone toward the pubis and the pubic bone toward the floor until you are "standing" on your pubic bone, with the weight on the legs and palms.

Alternatively, rather than pressing into the hands to lift your spine, just keep your elbows close to your ribs with the palms resting lightly on the floor, fingertips about level with the top of your shoulder. Exhaling, coil the spine deeply into the front body; slide the shoulder blades down the back, and from the tips of the shoulder blades, lift and open your upper chest. The deeper you coil the spine, the higher your hands will lift off the floor.

Remember, snakes have no hands. The lift and movement are all in the spine. Let your legs be part of your "tail."

Sustaining the Pose

Breathe deeply and slowly. Draw the shoulder blades down the back, lifting and opening the collarbones. As the curve of the upper spine deepens, it may be natural to take the head back; do this only if you can keep the back of the neck long. Lift the base of the skull toward the crown of the head. Firm the buttocks without clenching. Imagine you are holding the base of the tailbone with your muscles; imagine a ball of energy traveling up the spine from the tailbone to the skull.

Releasing the Pose

Exhale, bend the elbows, rest the forehead on the floor, relax the muscles. Repeat two or three times.

Points for Practice

Imagine spreading the base of the skull like a cobra's hood.

Practice taking the hands off the floor and letting the palms hover. You won't lift as high, but keep lengthening the neck; keep spreading your hood. Keep breathing. Feel the power of the breath to lift, elongate, and sustain you.

How does it feel to move from the breath and the spine?

What is it like to change perspective from flat on the earth to rising up—do you see differently, aspire differently?

Dance with your spine.

How is it to dance without using your legs? How is it to lift without using your arms?

What "poisons" would you like to neutralize through your yoga practice?

What does it mean to you to integrate the energy of your lower body with your head?

What would it feel like to be fully conscious, enlightened, and still be you?

What buried treasure or wisdom would you like to bring to light?

Shiva Bhairava, the beggar with dogs.

Shiva as Beggar
Downward and Upward Dog Poses

In much of India, dogs were long regarded as wild scavengers, something like coyotes in America. They were associated with the fringes of society, of questionable cleanliness and morals, loud-mouthed, clever in their way but not very trustworthy, first cousins to hyenas and jackals, and associated with cremation grounds.

By this way of thinking, dogs were natural companions for Shiva, who in his destructive and ascetic aspects is also found in remote spots such as cremation grounds, smeared with ash, accompanied by a troop of ghosts and goblins who are often described as "red-eyed from drinking *bhang*." (In modern parlance, *drinking bhang* equals *smoking dope*.) Lord of the Universe though he is, Shiva intentionally places himself outside the norm and surrounds himself with people or creatures who live far beyond the conventions of society. This, you will recall, was the basis of his conflict with King Daksha, who personified respect for social conventions and religious ritual at its most superficial levels.

Who is drawn to search for God or for the meaning of life? Not happy people in comfortable circumstances. As Bhairava, the beggar with the dog, Shiva represents the transcendent reality that seeks out people in desperate circumstances—social outcasts and the disenfranchised of all kinds.

However, in Nepal, Tibet, and neighboring parts of India, dogs are respected for their role as guardians and protectors. In some parts of Nepal, dogs are associated with the Mother Goddess, and even have their own special day during the fall festival of Dassehra. Some of the most famous cave temples in India, in Elephanta and Ellora, have lions guarding the entrance. These are not, however, the sleek lions of India, but creatures bearing a striking resemblance to Chinese or Tibetan Buddhist "lion dogs," those mythological creatures who guard temples and palaces in the snowy heights of the Himalayas where Shiva makes his home, as well as on the other side of the mountains in China.

Loyalty

One beautiful story involving a dog occurs at the very end of the *Mahabharata*. When the battle is lost and everyone they love is dead, the five Pandava brothers with their wife, Draupadi, set off on the Great Journey, walking north to the polar mountain of Heaven. They are led by the eldest brother, Yudhisthira, and accompanied by a dog who joins them and will not leave. One by one Yudhisthira's companions die along the way until only he and the dog are left to reach Heaven's door.

"You are welcome, Yudhisthira," says Indra, the Lord of Heaven, "but the dog can't come in."

"Then I can't either," says Yudhisthira. They argue; Indra points out that Yudhisthira has left everyone in his family behind, and that this is his opportunity to enjoy eternal bliss.

"They were dead," says Yudhisthira, "so I had to leave them behind. This dog is devoted to me; he had many opportunities to leave me, but he stayed. It is a sin against right conduct *(dharma)* to abandon one who is devoted to you, one who is terrified, or one who needs your protection. He is my companion. We have protected each other and comforted each other on this terrible journey, and as he has been loyal to me, I will not leave him."

With that, the dog is revealed to be an incarnation of Dharma himself, and both he and Yudhisthira enter the Heavenly realm.

So, like Shiva himself, who is at one and the same time Lord of the Universe, contemplative yogi, family man, and lover, and the war-like commander of scary troops of creatures from the burning ground, dogs are loyal guardians of kings and temples, trusted allies in war and hunting, playful companions, and dangerous outlaws who travel in packs. And in Indian culture, as in Persia, Greece, and Egypt, dogs are associated with death and the soul's journey home.

Downward Dog Pose *(adhomukhashvanasana)*

Embodying the Pose
Start on all fours, palms spread, hands in line with your shoulders. Tuck your toes. Inhale. Exhaling, lift the knees and roll your tailbone toward the ceiling. Widen through the shoulder blades. Let the weight of the head lengthen your neck toward the floor.

Sustaining the Pose
In the words of yoga teacher George Purvis, "Stretch your claws and pound your paws." Widen the hands, lengthen the fingers. Draw the shoulders down your back, and bring the lower tips of the shoulder blades toward the front body to open your collarbones and upper chest. Bend your knees slightly, then roll the sit bones up again. Notice if you are happier with your knees, hips, and ankles in one line, or with the knees slightly bent. Imagine your spine extends to form a tail. Stretch the tip of your tail back. Does this give you a sense of more length in the spine? Imagine that your tail curls like a chow's. Can you bring the tip of your tail to the rim of your sacrum? Does this enhance your feeling of lifting the sit bones? Does your dog work hard to stretch? Are you working hard in this pose, or can you find the place of rest inside it?

Releasing the Pose
Exhaling, come to all fours, bringing the weight evenly to both knees. Or, come out of the pose by walking the feet toward the hands until you are leaning over in a standing forward bend; then reach behind you, bring your hands to your buttocks, and on an exhalation, press the buttocks toward the floor to help lever your torso up to a standing position. Release your arms to your sides.

Upward Dog Pose *(urdhvamukhashvanasana)*

Embodying the Pose

From downward dog pose, broaden your hands and shoulder blades even more. Slide your shoulder blades down your back and lift your chest so much that your head begins to lift too. Exhaling, bring your pubic bone forward until your thighs are nearly parallel with the floor and the chest is lifting toward the vertical. Roll over the toes to bring the tops of your feet to the floor. Press down with the feet, lift the chest, and open the heart. If you like, smile and pant a little. Now where is your tail?

Sustaining the Pose

Follow your exhalation down your spine, lengthening the tail-bone away from the head. Lift the backs of the thighs toward the ceiling, and draw the center of your sacrum toward the earth. Soften your back ribs as you slide the tips of the shoulder blades down the back; pause, inhale, and slide your sternum toward your collarbones. Notice how you feel when you lift and open the structures that support your heart. Are you shortening or tightening your back ribs in an effort to lift the chest? Release them, and slide your rib cage toward your head like a bead on a string.

Remember how your dog's eyes look when he is happy; let your eyes reflect qualities of gladness, trust, happy expectation. Pay attention to the quality of your breath, especially in the back body; release any hardening in the lungs or ribs and let the strength of your arms, legs, and spine sustain you.

Points for Practice

If you have trouble sustaining your body weight on your arms, then rest the front of the thighs on the floor, or else change the angle of the entire pose to make it less challenging to the arms and wrists. One way to do this is to raise the level of the hands. For example, in upward dog pose, use the seat of a chair as your base instead of the floor; press down through the arms, lift the chest, and bring the pubic bone toward the edge of the chair. In downward dog pose, grounding the hands on a chair seat or on two blocks will shift more of the weight to the legs and allow you to lengthen through the arms and spine without over-straining your wrists and hands.

Some people prefer to practice upward dog pose with their toes tucked under and the balls of the feet on the floor, heels lifted; if you have very tight front ankles, this may be more comfortable than putting the tops of the feet on the floor. Try both positions with your feet; notice how foot placement affects the legs and hips. Play with different variations—your dog would.

Upward dog pose can resemble a low cobra pose—particularly if you keep your thighs down—but they are not at all the same pose. Think of the difference between dogs and snakes! Practice both poses, observing the way you use your spine, your arms, your legs, and your breath in each. Reflect that things that look similar outwardly may be quite different energetically.

Dogs are highly intuitive. Some people believe they can see spirits; and as any dog lover will tell you, they seem to have an almost psychic connection with the people they love. They are communal animals; relationships within their "pack" are important to dogs. They like to keep track of each others' welfare. Dogs love routine, making them role models for those of us who strive to maintain a daily practice. Dogs are excellent at "catching a scent" of something and following it, well, doggedly, until they find its origin, a procedure not unlike meditation. That quality of pursuing something steadily and not letting it drop, as Dharma in his dog form stayed with Yudhisthira through everything, recalls for me the *Yoga Sutra's* (1.12-15) discussion of *abhyasa* and *vairagya*, dedication and renunciation in practice. Read it for yourself and see what you think.

In both dog poses, you can feel the wonderful sensuality of being a dog and how exhilarating it feels to stretch your spine. As you open your chest between your arms, feel the strong, steady beat of your heart. Feel for the devotion in you that brings you back to your practice time after time. Something in us human beings is called to love and follow our inner teacher, as the dog accompanies Shiva or Yudhisthira. Maybe your body is like a dog, loyally going wherever you take it. Are you ever tempted to abandon it? How do you feel toward a person or being who loves and accepts you exactly as you are? Do you do that for yourself?

Do you listen to the dog in you who knows instinctively how it feels about things? How many things in your life right now make you want to grin and wag your tail and leap up and lick someone's face? Are there things in your life that make your inner dog wary? Are there areas of your dog nature that might need discipline? What if you thought about your yoga practice as training your dog?

Shiva meditating as the moon in his hair echoes the moon in the sky.

Why Shiva Has the Moon in His Hair

Half Moon Pose

One of Shiva's most beloved names is Chandrashekara (the One with the Moon in His Hair). The crescent moon rides like an ornament in his abundant, piled-up hair along with the river Ganga, snakes, and sometimes a skull—things can get pretty crowded at times. The moon, like the snake, is an ancient symbol of rebirth and regeneration. It stands for the passing, though cyclical, nature of time.

Indian cosmology is based on the concept of cycles coming into being, ending, and beginning again. This occurs on a cosmic macro-level, where one cycle can involve thousands of years, as well as on the observable, human micro-level. Shiva embodies the cosmic cycle; the moon represents the human cycle.

Creatures bound by the limitations of physical existence are bound by time. Shiva is not. Shiva represents the formlessness out of which all forms arise. When a cycle ends, cosmic or individual, its elements are reabsorbed into him, only to be reformed and re-created like a new moon manifesting in the night sky.

When I was very young, not yet four, I had a small tiger stuffed with sawdust that was my favorite toy. My family lived near International House in upper Manhattan, Columbia University's residence for international students and visiting faculty. Someone had a full-sized tiger skin in his room on the ground floor; you could see it clearly as you walked by. I derived an enormous feeling of satisfaction from taking my toy tiger to visit the tiger skin. I would hold my tiger up to see the skin, and a deep sense of symmetry filled my soul. There I was with my small child-sized tiger, and there in that big high-ceilinged room was an enormous tiger, which I somehow recognized as "real." I saw the big tiger, and the big tiger, I felt, saw me and my small tiger. Microcosm, macrocosm.

This, in a nutshell, is the sense of the Sanskrit word *darshana:* you see God, or an image that represents the divine to you, and you *are seen.* A child's poem says, "I see the moon, the moon sees me; God bless the moon, and God bless me." The moon in the sky and I here on earth exist in relationship to one another. The blessing arrives with recognition of the relationship.

How did the moon come to be caught in Shiva's hair? It was one of the results of churning the Ocean of Milk. At the very beginning of this cycle of time, the *devas* (good angels) and *asuras* (rebel angels) joined forces to churn the Ocean of Milk in quest of *amrita,* the nectar of immortality. Mount Meru served as the churning stick and the serpent Vasuki as the churning rope. Vishnu—the Sustainer of the Universe, you'll recall—took the form of a tortoise to hold the mountain in place on his back and prevent it from sinking into the sea. All sorts of treasures came up as they churned: Lakshmi, the Goddess of Wealth, who married Vishnu; Kamadhenu, the Wish-Fulfilling Cow; Chandra, the moon; and, unexpectedly, a deadly poison mist arose, which burned everyone's eyes and lungs and threatened to destroy all of life before they had even discovered the amrita. Saving them all, Shiva inhaled the poison mist and held it in his throat so as not to swallow it. But even the Lord of the Universe is affected by his actions; he was strong enough that the poison couldn't kill him, but it burned his throat terribly, staining the skin permanently dark blue.

Out of gratitude, and to cool the burning, the moon came to live in his hair. The devas and asuras did discover the nectar of immortality, but that is another story.

Half Moon Pose *(ardhachandrasana)*

Embodying the Pose

Stand with your back about six inches from a wall. Exhaling, step or jump your feet wide apart. Inhaling, lift your arms to shoulder height. Exhaling, turn your right leg out from the hip. Exhaling, bring your right hand to the floor, or to a block, in line with your shoulder; as your bottom hand descends to the floor, maintain the lift of the upper arm and hand toward the ceiling. Coming into the pose this way is like doing half a cartwheel. As your right arm comes down, your left leg naturally lifts, doesn't it? Bring the left foot in line with the hip, and reach through both legs from the core of your belly to the heels. One foot moves into the floor; the other foot moves into space. Lengthen the spine. Lean your upper back and shoulder blades toward the wall. Turn your head to look toward the ceiling. Draw both shoulder blades forward, toward the sternum, to open your top chest and collarbones. Imagine the ends of your lifted foot and your lifted hand as the horns of the crescent moon. Visualize sending beams of light from your fingers and toes into the sky.

Sustaining the Pose

Check your distance from the wall. If you are too close, you may push yourself forward; if you are too far away, leaning back will feel strained. You are looking for a place where the body feels supported, light, free of strain and effort.

Practice the pose a foot away from the wall or in the middle of the room. Can you lean back on space with the same feeling of assurance that you had with a wall behind you? Is there a point where your back body "knows" that there is a wall behind it even though they are not touching?

For most people, the back body is deeply unconscious. We never see it directly, and we have to know it through feeling and intuition. Does using the wall heighten your awareness of what's going on back there?

Does it feel restricted?

How is the hip on your lifted leg? If it cramps, then you are probably trying to hold up the leg from the outer edge. Can you lift the inner thigh on that leg to support the outer thigh?

Where is your head? Draw an imaginary line from the crown of your head to your hip to your foot on the lifted leg. Are they on the same level?

Notice your breathing. Where do you notice your breath most clearly?

Imagine this pose as a totality, as if you were exhaling equally through all your pores, even the ones on your face and head. Does this make you feel lighter?

Releasing the Pose

Take three breaths, then, exhaling, stretch your lifted foot back to meet the floor. Feel how your body regains its upright posture from this action. Exhaling, release the arms to your sides.

Points for Practice

What holds you up? Is it really the wall? Find the dynamic play between the lifted foot and the grounded foot, the lifted arm and the grounded arm.

What holds the moon up? Imagine yourself as the moon hanging in the sky. What sustains you? How do you feel when you see the moon unexpectedly?

What cycles in your life do you notice through your yoga practice? Most of us experience times when we feel enthusiastic and eager to hit the mat, interspersed with periods when the whole enterprise feels stale, uninspired, the same old thing. As on the mat, so in life. What gets you through the stale times till renewal comes? Devotion? Stubbornness? Faith? Sheer momentum? Are you willing to honor your personal phases, or do you feel a need to override them?

Archaeologists now believe that the first calendars were invented by women, who noticed that their own menstrual cycles were similar to the moon's and kept track of events accordingly. Do you think your body has a sense of time and timing, regardless of whether you are a menstruating woman? Do you ever just know in your body that "the time has come" for something?

Journaling

Have you ever had an experience of darshana—feeling seen by, in essential relationship with, some thing that seemed to be one with you and yet far bigger than you? Write about that. If you have not yet had that experience, write about what it might be like to have it.

Shiva catches Ganga on his head.
He is admired by Parvati, Nandi,
and the sage Bhaghiratha.

How the River Ganga Fell to Earth

Waterfall Pose

If you look closely at Shiva's hair, you will see a small female figure there with a stream of water coming from her mouth. This is the goddess Ganga and this is how she came to be there.

A very long time ago there was a prince named Bhagiratha. His great-great-grandfather Sagara was the king of Ayodhya; some people say he was the thirteenth ancestor of Lord Rama. Sagara was the father of sixty thousand sons. He was a great king who wanted to be even greater. He performed the Horse Sacrifice, in which a horse was set free to roam as far as he could without being stopped; if the horse's progress went unopposed, the king who owned him was understood to be the ruler of all territories covered by the horse. Ninety-nine times Sagar performed this ceremony, and each time his territory increased. When he began preparations for the hundredth sacrifice, Lord Indra grew alarmed that Sagar's holdings would impinge on Heaven itself. Who knows?—he might even oust Indra from his throne. So Indra stole the horse.

Since Sagar ruled most of the earth, Indra hid the horse in Patala, the underground realm. As it happened, the sage Kapila Muni had his hermitage in Patala, and he was sitting in a deep meditative trance under a tree near the spot where Indra tethered the horse. When the theft became known, all but one of Sagar's sons went to look for the horse. Finally they traced it to Patala; and, seeing Kapila Muni and no one else in the vicinity, they jumped to the conclusion that he was the thief and began to beat him. It can be very dangerous even to touch a yogi who is in a trance; the powerful energies in his body are apt to "ground" themselves in you, just as if you caught hold of a wire carrying electrical current. When the princes attacked Kapila Muni, the startled sage's third eye flew open. He cursed the disturbance and its agents, and, in seconds, the sixty thousand sons were burnt to ash.

When an action is unleashed, its effects cannot be reversed, but they may be mitigated by fresh actions; this is the law of karma. Kapila could not take back the destruction of Sagar's sons, nor could they make amends for having disturbed him. It was left to their family members to make amends and free the sixty thousand souls from their cursed state of disembodiment. Unable to recall his curse, Kapila added a condition: The sons of Sagar would be free to reincarnate when their souls were cleansed by the water of Mother Ganga.

Sagar became a forest hermit, leaving the kingdom to his one remaining son, Ansuman, who apologized to Kapila. First Ansuman, then his son Dilip, and finally Dilip's son Bhagiratha performed penance for their ancestors' terrible error and prayed for divine forgiveness. For generations, the children of that family offered up the fruits of their austerities. And, since no action is ever really lost, the family's efforts gradually accumulated good results. When Bhagiratha became a yogi, the sincerity, fervor, and duration of his practice at last won the full support of Heaven.

Now at that time, Ganga existed only in celestial form. As the goddess Ganga, she appeared as the River of Heaven, or the Milky Way. The error of Bhagiratha's ancestors required her intervention, so Ganga was requested by the gods to visit Earth for the job. (You will notice, if you read enough Indian mythology, that when a problem is really insoluble, the Goddess is often called in.) Ganga was reluctant but drew on her infinite compassion for ignorant humanity to say, "I'll go, but you know, I am so powerful that if I fall to Earth without anything to contain me, the force of my fall will destroy it entirely. One of you will have to catch me." Who was strong enough and stable enough to catch and channel the full onslaught of feminine energy? Only Shiva, whose station is the peak of Mount Kailash, the highest mountain and nearest to Heaven. Shiva offered to catch her on his head, where his long, tangled, matted hair would provide channels for the river and allow her to distribute her power so no one stream would overwhelm the Earth. They worked out the details; Ganga leaped, Shiva caught her, and the force of her fall carried her easily into the underworld where Bhagiratha's ancestors were liberated instantly when her water touched their ashes.

Ganga developed a motherly affection for the souls on Earth and took on a permanent manifestation as the river Ganga. Her source is at Gangotri, near Mount Kailash; from there, it is said, she divides into a hundred streams until she forms a delta and joins the ocean near the Bay of Bengal. Ultimately, as the source of all the rivers, they as well as water-dwelling creatures within them are her "children." Today many people hope to die on her banks in India so their ashes can more easily join with her waters; and even far away from India, there is something deeply comforting about consigning a loved one's ashes to the water. Just as all rivers are Ganga, so all rivers flow to the ocean where all life began.

Waterfall Pose *(viparita karani)*

Embodying the Pose

Place a sticky mat with the narrow end at the wall. Put a bolster with the long edge next to the wall, but not quite touching; allow about six inches of distance. Fold a blanket, and place it at a right angle to the bolster; this is for your shoulders and head.

Sit on the edge of the bolster, with the outside of your right arm touching the wall. Now lie down onto your left side. Scoot back on the bolster until your sit bones touch the wall. Now, exhaling, swing your legs up to the right and your shoulders to the left. You should now be lying with your sacrum and the back of your pelvis on the bolster, legs up the wall, shoulders and head on the blanket. Bring your arms to shoulder height, bend the elbows, and point your fingers in the direction of your head. The palms should be facing up.

Sustaining the Pose

Draw your tailbone lightly toward the floor and feel the tops of the thighbones settling into the backs of the hip sockets. If your tailbone is unable to drop, you may be a little too close to the wall; check the distance of your props as well as the position of your body. The belly should be more or less parallel with the ceiling. The pubic bone should be able to roll down, toward the floor.

If your arms are uncomfortable, try moving them up or down a little. If your forearms are lifted so you must bend the wrists to bring the backs of the hands to the floor, place a folded cloth or an eyebag under the forearms and wrists. Notice if this promotes a sense of the upper arm moving toward the back of the shoulder sockets (i.e., toward the floor).

Your forehead should be just a little higher than your chin, inviting the gaze to turn downward and inward. Close the eyes, or use an eyebag if you are comfortable with a slight weight on your eyes. Soften the palms, let the brain slide away from the forehead toward the base of the skull, and observe your breathing.

You may belt the legs with a strap halfway between the hips and the knees, or put a sandbag on the soles of the feet. Either of these interventions serves to stabilize the legs.

Releasing the Pose

When you have been here long enough, exhale and slide the soles of the feet down the wall. If you are on a bolster, lift the hips and move the bolster out from underneath you. Bring your hips to the floor. Then roll to the side and use the strength of your arms to bring yourself back to a seated position.

Points for Practice

With your legs up the wall and your arms overhead, imagine the flow of a powerful healing force that enters your toes, flows through your legs and pelvis into your torso, into your chest, back, and arms, your neck, your head. Like a river, let it pick up and carry away whatever tension and detritus are stuck in your body. Feel the flow of your blood, a tiny personal river, and the flow of energy in the body along similar channels. Be willing to let go of whatever in you is impeding your natural progression to the ocean. What do you want to hold onto?

Where is the line between letting go and giving up? Reflect that there are things we cannot release by our own efforts, but that our efforts may be the very thing that invites divine intervention. Notice the quality of effort in your legs. Do you try to hold them up with your breath, your muscles, your mind? Where is the minimum of effort that lets the femur heads drop to the floor while the flesh and skin rise toward the ceiling?

Imagine yourself as a conduit for a powerful healing energy that starts somewhere out in the Milky Way and travels through your body, draining into the imaginary ocean surrounding your head and hands. Imagine yourself embodying the continent of India, with your feet at Ganga's source in the Himalayas, your flanks the mountain slopes, your chest and belly the plains, and your head and hands the coast and seashore.

Notice your breathing. Positioned as you are, the diaphragm has gravity's cooperation in moving up on the exhalation, so you are likely to find your outbreath becoming particularly effortless. Can you feel the lungs releasing into the curve of the ribs? Does one drop, or spread, more or faster than the other? Which is the reluctant lung? Stay in this pose up to 20 minutes if you are comfortable. If you become uncomfortable, is your mind getting restless, or is it the body telling you it's been there long enough?

This is an inversion, a pose in which the belly is higher than the heart. It is a supported alternative to shoulderstand. Overall, its effect tends to be cooling, calming, and relaxing, but be aware of your own responses. If you feel pressure in the eyes or head, if it bothers your neck or back to be in this position, if you have trouble breathing due to a cold or sinus congestion, consider simply resting flat on the floor with your legs up the wall, or check with an experienced yoga teacher to see if your props are the right height and configuration for you. Generally, inversions are not recommended for menstruating women or for anyone with glaucoma or a hiatal hernia.

Arjuna won the hand of Princess
Draupadi at this unusual archery contest.

Shiva's Bow

Bow Pose

One of Shiva's forms is that of an aboriginal hunter. His weapon of choice is the bow, which figures in other stories as a symbol of divine power that can become available to us if we prepare ourselves to handle it. A story in the famous, beloved epic *Mahabharata* provides an example.

Once upon a time, so long ago as to be almost mythical, Duryodhana, an aggressive and morally inferior man, gained leadership of the kingdom of Ayodhya through trickery. The rightful rulers, the five Pandava brothers, were exiled to the forest for twelve years. Many of their people followed them, begging them to stay. The brothers declined, saying the right thing to do was to accept what had happened and to plan their strategies for the future.

They knew that eventually there might be a war. Each brother practiced his own special skill as a spiritual discipline. They lived simply, like forest ascetics, or athletes in training. They ate sparingly, dressed plainly, and found a certain relief in their distance from political intrigue. They had plenty of time to perfect their warrior skills, their balance, their silence, their breath, their focus, their subtle control of finer muscles. It was in many ways a happy time, except for the reports reaching them of how the people suffered—the poor were not protected, the sick uncared for, and the wealthy and powerful abused their privilege more shamelessly every day.

Concentration

When Arjuna and his cousin, Duryodhana, were students, Arjuna won an archery contest designed by the master teacher Dronacharya. Setting up a wooden bird in a tree across the river as the target, Dronacharya asked each student to come up, one by one, to take a turn to shoot it down.

"Describe the target," Dronacharya challenged each student.

The first said, "I see a tree with a bird in it; I see the branch, the leaves, the bird's body, and in the center of the bird's head, an eye. That is the target."

Dronacharya remained silent.

The second said, "I see a bird and in the head, an eye."

Still Dronacharya remained silent.

Arjuna said, "I see the eye in the center of the bird's head."

"Shoot!" said Dronacharya.

Of the five Pandava brothers, Arjuna was the best archer. His focus was legendary, and his strength almost superhuman. If Arjuna had lived in the old American West, he might have been the kind of gunman who can toss a penny up in the air and drill it clean through the center before it hit the ground. But he was no picker of fights. He and his brothers would much rather have remained in the forest than have gone to the battlefield. However, they could not shirk their duty and their obligation to the kingdom that was rightfully theirs.

Heaven itself supported the Pandavas' cause. The gods remember what we often forget, that spirit is indestructible; that death comes to all bodies eventually; that a warrior's destiny is to uphold justice and protect the people; and that when we fulfill our destiny without attachment or aversion, no real harm is done. Heaven's position was not to get so ego-entangled that you start a war, but if you must defend the ones you are responsible for, do it wholeheartedly and without rancor. The gods looked at the Pandavas and wondered when they would act.

Shiva was eager to give Arjuna his bow, which no one but himself or a true hero could draw. However, the rules of chivalry required Arjuna to claim it as his own, to embrace his destiny as a hero. Shiva couldn't just say, "Here, take my bow." And he was getting tired of waiting for Arjuna to ask.

So, snickering a little, Shiva put on his form as a Kirata (a tribal hunter) dressed in animal skins and carrying a bow. He changed his wife Parvati into a Kirati, with her own smaller bow, and together they went to sneak up on Arjuna.

Arjuna was deep in the forest, standing in a clearing performing yogic austerities to attract Shiva's grace. Balanced on one leg in tree pose, arms raised, he stood silent, rooted, breathing slowly in the filtered sunlight. His peripheral vision had become as wide as the clearing itself. Something stirred on the edge of his sight, and unbelievably, here in the clearing, a wild boar came charging. His mind too still for thought, he instinctively drew his bow, shot true, and the boar dropped.

When he checked the boar, he found two arrows in it, points nearly touching—his from the front and another from behind. Who? Looking up, he saw a dark-skinned, tribal hunter, his hair done in a topknot, dressed in filthy hides, with his lady beside him; they stood proprietarily over the boar and their faces were not friendly. You can imagine the dialogue:

"What do you think you're doing here? I was here first."

"That was my boar. I shot first."

"Well *you* shot from behind."

Till finally—and this was what Shiva wanted—Arjuna said the equivalent of "Well, draw, partner!" challenging him to a shootout, and it was standoff time in the forest.

They shot till their clothing was shredded by the arrows' friction, till the shafts were splintered, till at last Arjuna's magic, inexhaustible quiver was somehow exhausted. Then the dark hunter picked up a handful of dust and blew it in his opponent's face. Arjuna fell with a small cry, lifting his hand . . . When he came to, he was on the ground, and standing over him were Shiva and Parvati, grinning. "My Lord!" said Arjuna.

"My friend!" said Shiva.

"Are you sure you're all right?" said Parvati.

And that is how Arjuna accepted the gift of Shiva's bow and set off back to his family's camp to tell them the time had come to prepare for war. The story of that war is too long and complicated to tell here; but when it began, and Arjuna was on the battlefield facing the opposing army, his heart failed him for a moment. He had Shiva's bow, and Lord Krishna was his charioteer. His cause was just; but when he saw all the individuals who were going to die in that war and thought of all the suffering that was about to be unleashed, he threw down his bow and said, "I won't fight. It's not worth it. He can have the damn kingdom."

Then Krishna spoke, and what he said to Arjuna is famous today as the *Bhagavad Gita*, the *Song of God;* it is one of the world's most beloved treatises on yoga and the life of the Spirit. One thing that has stayed with me since I first heard it forty years ago is this: Whatever I do, I must do without attachment, offering the action and its results to God. And if I honestly do my best 100 percent, and leave the results to God, the consequences, whatever they are, are in God's hands.

Bow Pose *(dhanurasana)*

Embodying the Pose

There is more than one way to take the shape of a strung bow, but let's try the simple downward-facing bow.

Lie on your stomach with your legs hip-width apart, feet pointing back. Rest your forehead on the floor. Bend your knees. Exhaling, roll your shoulders back and grasp your ankles. Inhale, and wait. Exhaling, move the front of the ankles strongly into the hands, lift the knees, and raise the legs and the chest off the floor. The arms and hands act like a bowstring to make the body taut like a bent bow. Lift the head. Rest the weight on the abdomen, not on the hipbones or ribs.

Sustaining the Pose

The action of the pose comes from the steady strength of the legs, balanced by the firm grip of the hands and the ability of the chest and shoulders to open. Your lower back will bend because the legs are working strongly. Don't try to create the bend by compressing your lumbar spine (back waist area); keep the spine itself as long as possible. That includes the neck; lift the base of your skull to balance the lift of your breastbone.

Your breathing will be quick because the abdomen is extended, but breathe as smoothly as you can. Let the breath be the string that connects the elements of effort and release in the pose.

Releasing the Pose

Exhale, release the ankles, straighten the legs, bring the head and limbs back to the floor, stack one hand over the other, rest your forehead on the hands, and relax.

Points for Practice

Where do you experience opening? Where do you experience constriction? Where do you find the balance between the pull of the upper body and the resistance of the lower body? Between the front body and the back body? Where does your strength come from?

Where is your focus? What "de-focuses" you most strongly?

Is your body an adequate vehicle for the power you have? Are you straining in this pose? What would it feel like to be this strong and stretched and relaxed at the same time?

Be aware of your breath. Is the back of your throat open or closed?

How do you feel physically? What parts of your body are you most aware of now?

How do you feel emotionally? Does this shape leave you feeling empowered or defeated? Did you use your strength well? Do you think it's likely that, while you are working to perfect yourself, some benevolent higher power—like Shiva in the story—is secretly encouraging you to do just that? Are you more likely to rise to a challenge if you feel you're not the only one who will benefit? When we do the right thing, are we ever the only ones to benefit? How do you know when the time has come for you to act? How do you act without wanting to own the results?

Dharma is the principle of right conduct. Krishna reminds Arjuna that, as a warrior prince, it is his dharma, his duty and responsibility, to fight against the willful perversion of power. What do you think is your dharma?

नन्दीश्वर

Shiva as Nandi's Lord.

Shiva and His Bull, Nandi
Cow Face Pose

The cow is a powerful symbol in Indian culture; cows, as you may know, are considered sacred. This is natural if you recall India's ancient pastoral culture. To nomadic herders, even settled farmers, cows represent wealth, status, even life itself. Look at the modern Masai people in Africa, or read some ancient Irish epics, such as the *Cattle Raid of Cooley,* for a global sense of how other cultures feel about their cattle.

So, in India, cows represent all that is nourishing, maternal, generous, life-giving, bountiful, good. Shiva's vehicle and chief animal companion is Nandi, the bull, who is both strong and virile and a legendary devotee and servant. Nandi is often shown carrying Shiva and Parvati on his back across the universe, or more prosaically, giving their children rides as the family makes its way down from their mountain home. In every Shiva temple the door is guarded by an image of Nandi, so placed that if you stand just right you can look between his horns and see Shiva in his aniconic *lingam* (pillar) form.

Rivers, especially the Indus, are sometimes said to be cows because of the way they nourished Indian culture along their banks. If you think of it, there is something about a calm, rolling river, stocked with fish and water plants, home to birds, a drinking place for animals and people, even a means of transportation, that does resemble the qualities of a cow. Indian people use all the products of the cow. They drink her milk and turn it into butter, cheese, or sweets. They cook with *ghee* (clarified butter), burn it in lamps, and use it as medicine. Village people use dung for fuel and building material—mixed with mud, it makes fine bricks; mixed with water, it produces a smooth, odorless, antiseptic covering for dirt floors. Of course, they use the bullocks' strength and stamina for cultivating the fields and drawing water, for pulling carts, even riding. When a cow dies of old age, her hide may be used to make sandals.

When the river Ganga fell to the earth, the place she landed in the Himalayas formed a glacier. Today it is known as Bhagirathi Glacier, after the king, you remember, whose yogic penances attracted her grace and Shiva's; and it is a place of pilgrimage. The glacier itself has peaks that look a little like a cow's ears; but most important, there is an opening out of which the river Ganga flows. It is remarkable that she comes from this opening already a river, not a tiny trickle like some young rivers, but already mature. Pilgrims go to pray there, bathe in her water at the source, and take it home with them—and it is a fact that Ganga water can remain in a closed container for years without turning scummy or going bad. This opening in the glacier is called Gaumukh (the Cow's Mouth), bringing together the ideas of cow and river as a life-giving mother.

Before turning to the cow face pose, I want to tell you a story about cows. This is an old Indian story, and there are many versions, but this is the way I remember it being told to me.

Once there was a Brahmin who had four sons. When the time came for him to die, he instructed his sons that they were to divide his property absolutely equally. "No problem," said the sons. "And if there's anything left over," said the dying man, "you'll have to eat it! Agreed?" What could they say? A dying parent's wish is sacred. They agreed.

The old man was not hugely wealthy, and the sons were all men of integrity, so they managed to divide the clothing, the household goods, what money there was, without much difficulty. But the cattle! There were eleven cows. To divide them equally would give each son two and three-quarters cows, and, obviously, that wouldn't work. You'd have to cut up the cows. It's nearly as great a sin to kill a cow as to disobey a Brahmin's dying wish, and to eat the remaining cow's flesh is maybe even worse than killing a Brahmin. I suppose you might have sold them and divided the money, but in this story that was not an option; anyway, these were particular cows, their father's cows.

What to do?

One son, or maybe it was a daughter, had an idea: they would ask the holy man who meditated in a cave outside the village.

"Simple," said the holy man. "I have one cow. I will give you my cow. Now you have twelve cows. Divide them equally, you each have four cows. Then one of you will give me back my cow. The cows have been divided equally, your father's wish is carried out, nobody has to kill or eat a cow."

"No, no," said the sons, "we should each give you a cow, then we will each have three cows and you will be richer by three cows. It's the least we can do to repay you."

"Fine," said the holy man, "I accept. But you know, you're only giving me back what is mine already, just as you are mine. Don't you recognize me?"

"Pashupati! Shiva!" they all exclaimed and fell lovingly at his feet.

According to the man who told me this story, God, or your spirituality, is the twelfth cow. When you have an impossible decision to make in life, when things do not add up, always remember to bring your sense of higher power into the equation, and your difficulties will be solved.

Cow Face Pose *(gomukhasana)*

Embodying the Pose

In the full pose, you sit equally on both sit bones, knees stacked one over the other, feet beside your hips. If you look down at your knees, you can imagine a cow's face looking up at you, with your legs and feet as the horns, or ears. Keep the legs and feet active, grounding you; you will feel some stretch in your outer hips.

Keeping the spine lifting out of the grounding of the pelvis, inhale and lift your arms overhead. Bend one elbow and reach that hand behind your head, bringing the palm to the area between your shoulder blades. Reach the other arm out to the side at shoulder height, rotate it till the palm faces up, then on an exhalation bring that arm behind you with the back of your hand against your back, palm facing out. Exhaling, rotate the inner edges of both shoulder blades toward the spine.

Stop and check the sensation in your shoulders. If there is no pain, slide the upper hand down your back and the lower hand up your back until the fingertips touch; moving slowly and with awareness, continue until you can clasp the fingers of the two hands together; or, if you have long arms and open shoulders, even clasp the wrists. You will have one elbow up, one elbow down, with your chest in the middle, like a cow's face with one ear up and one ear down. If your right knee is on top, then your left arm is raised. If your left knee is on top, then the right arm is raised.

Sustaining the Pose

If your hands do not immediately clasp—and if not, welcome to the club—then hold a yoga strap or an old necktie in your upper hand as you are coming into the pose. Your lower hand can grasp the end of the strap, and as your shoulders open, you will walk your hands closer together until some day you will dispense with the strap. Or not. Whatever you are clasping, the work is to find openness and ease in this pose.

Relax the throat and breathe fully, all the way into the pelvis. Use the muscles of your back to lengthen the spine and neck and draw the inner edges of the shoulder blades toward the spine, creating space in the shoulder socket. Use the breath to create inner space in the tight places. Breathe into your armpits.

Keep the feet and hips firm. As you rotate the arms in the shoulders, rotate the thighs in the hips. You are creating a very firm, focused line of energy in your midline, with the arms and legs opening away from it by, paradoxically, moving toward it. Are your knees O.K.? Do your feet touch the floor? Do you have any judgments about your body's flexibility? Are you patient with its limitations?

Watch your mind. What does it do? Do you get anxious when your arms are twisted behind your back? Are there elements of this position that feel coerced? Are you inclined to force yourself deeper into difficult places? How comfortable are you with breathing and waiting for more space to develop?

Watch your eyes, your face, your jaw, your breath. Where in this pose do you find the calmness, the flowing quality, the generous giving nature of a river or a cow?

Releasing the Pose

Exhaling, release the arms and bring them to your sides. Uncross your legs. Stand up, or lie down, a moment, returning your body to a familiar sense of symmetry. How do you feel?

Points for Practice

This is a complex pose. The top half and the bottom half are both asymmetrical. How do your shoulders feel? How do your hips feel? What is your overall body sense? Are you distracted from an overall awareness by the intensity of sensation in one part? Try moving your awareness from quadrant to quadrant until your chest and hips, arms and legs are all fully present in your consciousness.

Journaling

How do you respond to the "Twelfth Cow" story? Can you recall a time in your life when a seemingly insoluble situation was resolved in such an "outside the box" way?

Affirmation: There is a twelfth cow.

Markandeya holds tight to the Shiva lingam as Shiva breaks his bond with Death.

Escaping Bondage
Noose Pose

Pasha in Sanskrit means "a noose, or a fetter"; *pashu* means "cattle," or by extension a "bound being". The looped rope, or lariat, is part of a hunter's basic gear because it can be used to snare an animal or transport it. The looped rope is associated in Indian mythology with Yama, Lord of Death, who uses it to drag off reluctant souls, and with Vishnu, who used it to bind transgressors against *dharma* with the fetters of illness, madness, misfortune.

As cattle are restrained by a lariat, human beings may be bound by *avidya*, spiritual ignorance. Avidya is the principle of radical ignorance that leads us to mistake bondage for freedom, the unimportant for the important, the transitory for the eternal, things of small and transitory worth for things of ultimate and eternal value.

On the other hand, we may choose to bind ourselves to the principles *(yamas* and *niyamas)* and disciplines of yoga. Life as a human being involves binding of one kind or another, until we transcend all bindings to realize ourselves as eternal and none other than God. In the system of raja yoga, the whole endeavor is to disentangle your consciousness from its false sense of identification.

> I am not mind, intellect, ego, nor field of consciousness;
>   neither hearing, smelling, sight, nor taste.
> I am not speech, hands, or feet, nor am I the organs
>   of reproduction or excretion.
> I am not *dharma*, not purpose, not liberation, not desire.
> I am not sin, happiness, or suffering.
> I am neither the enjoyer nor the enjoyed; neither death, fear,
>   nor social class; neither father nor mother, nor friend,
>   nor teacher, nor student.
> My nature is the bliss of pure consciousness.
> *Shivo'ham.* I am Shiva.

This much-loved song by Shankaracharya takes the devotee through a process of non-identification with all that binds us to our idea of being someone in particular, replacing that mistaken identity with an assertion of the truth: *Shivo'ham.* I am Shiva.

Shiva is called Pashupati, Lord of Beasts, meaning the one with the noose. In the Kannada language of South India, *pashu* means both "cow or bull" and "creature or creation." *Pati* means "lord, creator." And *pasam* means "the relationship between the Lord and the creation, or the creatures." Like the Good Shepherd of Judaeo-Christian imagery, Pashupati is in the world to throw his lariat and bring back wandering members of the herd to safety. He helps to bind us to the pursuit of yoga and to the things that ultimately lead us safely away from the suffering of ignorance to the unlimited bliss that is our real nature.

Pasha thus has a double meaning. It is the thing that binds us, whether to ignorance or to wisdom, and the means of our liberation from binding. Often we are the last to notice how tightly we have wound ourselves up in some situation, and, like a vehicle stuck in the mud, it takes an expert with firm footing on solid ground to pull us out.

Another story from Shiva's myths tells of his devotee Markandeya, who was fated to die at age sixteen. When Death arrived to catch him in his noose, Markandeya wrapped his arms around Shiva's image and held on. Shiva emerged from the lingam to claim Markandeya as his own, and Death had to give up his claim.

Noose Pose *(pashasana)*

Embodying the Pose

Squat on the floor, flatfooted if you can; if not, support your heels with a folded sticky mat. Keep the knees and feet together. Lift your sit bones off the floor. Exhaling, turn the torso to the right, till your left armpit comes to the outside of your right knee. Now bring your left knee slightly forward to maximize the twist. Exhaling, extend the left arm from the shoulder. Exhaling again, turn the arm around the right leg. Bending the left elbow toward the left leg, bring your hand near your left hip. Now, exhale and extend the right arm from the shoulder, bring it behind your back, bend the right elbow, and clasp the fingers of the left hand with the right hand.

Sustaining the Pose

Exhaling, twist the spine to the right, turn your head to look over your right shoulder. After a few breaths, turn and look over the left shoulder. Keep the calves firm, and keep the ribs as close as possible to the thighs. Breathe normally. Stay for 30 to 60 seconds.

If your hands do not readily clasp, use a yoga strap. If you are twisting to the right, begin with the strap in your left hand and trail the end behind you as you bring that arm around; then when you reach back with the right arm, catch the end of the strap.

Adapting the Pose

Even if you cannot squat or cannot come anywhere close to clasping your hands around your legs in this twist, you can experience something of the shape of the pose. Sit in a chair. Elevate your feet on a block or stool so that your knees and legs can come close to your chest. Make a large loop with your yoga strap. Slip it over both legs, near the groin. Exhaling, bring your right arm around behind you; catch the strap with your fingers or hand. Now, exhaling, reach your left arm from the shoulder and bring it to the outside of your right knee. Exhaling, bend your left elbow if possible, or press the left forearm into the outside of the right knee. Use the fingers of the left hand to draw the strap down and to the right over your knee; use the fingers of the right hand to draw the strap to the right behind the back; draw the right shoulder blade forward, and open your chest.

Where in your body do you try to force this twist—in your shoulders, belly, jaw, eyes?

What emotions arise when your breathing feels restricted?

What arises in your body or mind when your arm is twisted behind your back?

In a twist, when the body's parts are not in their usual relation, do you get confused? Does confusion move you toward ignorance, or toward awareness?

If you cannot squat, or cannot reach around readily to clasp your hands, what do you tell yourself about yourself? Do physical restrictions mean you are inadequate, or bad? Is it all right to use props, or otherwise adapt the pose to your body? Do you celebrate what you can do or ignore it to focus on your shortcomings?

If this pose is hard for you, do you want to just not do it? Is that O.K.?

Try initiating the twist from your navel. From your breath. From your tailbone.

Try initiating the twist from your internal organs. Do they like the deep internal massage?

In *pashasana* you create your own noose out of your arms, closely binding the legs to the body in a twist. Where is the freedom in this pose? In the breath? In the willingness to restrain yourself, to hold yourself to something difficult? In experiencing that you created this particular binding, and you can release it?

Leaving aside how it might look to an outside observer, what is the true shape of your pose?

Releasing the Pose

Release the clasp of hands or belt, exhale, twist to the other side. Finally, on an exhalation, unclasp, release the torso back to the center, sit on the floor and extend the legs.

Points for Practice

If it's true that what we do in our asana practice we do elsewhere in life, then maybe this pose has something to teach us about self-created restrictions. To what, or to whom, do you choose to bind yourself? Is it possible to live with no bindings of any kind?

Can you think of a time when you were so lost or stuck—physically, spiritually, emotionally, whatever—that you didn't know how to proceed and someone or something came along and freed you? Did you welcome that intervention at the time? Are there any areas of your life where you might do well to restrain yourself but find it difficult? How do you feel about making things easier for yourself? What do you value more in a guide—someone who encourages you to take things at a comfortable pace, or someone who goads you to do more than you think you can?

Look at the "nooses" in the illustration: Death's noose reaching for the boy, Shiva's arms around him, and the boy's arms around the Shiva lingam. What are the things that threaten to "grab" you from your practice? What pulls you back? What do you cling to most strongly?

Journaling

Using Shankaracharya's song as a model *(I am not this, I am not that . . . Shivo'ham. I am Shiva)*, write your own manifesto stating what you are not and what you ultimately are.

Mother Kali in her fierce aspect stands on Shiva's corpse.

A Meditation on Death

Corpse Pose

Today in the West, many of us go through most of our lives without ever seeing a dead body. Death has become unfamiliar, the domain of experts; as a culture we prefer it when people die in an antiseptic medical setting, where there are doctors who can pronounce them officially dead, and the undertakers will come quickly to pick up the body. We debate whether or not it is good to let children see people when they have died, but have not yet been made to look "natural" by the experts at the funeral home. Even adults have full cultural permission to declare themselves too upset or sensitive to be in the same room with a corpse. We are apt to regard death as a failure, an embarrassment, an injustice, something that shouldn't happen to anyone except people we dislike. Religious people are something of an exception, finding solace in the conviction of heaven for their beloved dead, but then, of course, there are all the rest of us who may or may not qualify for a particular heaven. . . . As a hospice volunteer, later a hospital chaplain, I have had many opportunities to witness the ways people respond to death, and I am here to tell you that rarely is it with much in the way of calm acceptance.

Before things got so compartmentalized, this was not true in America. People died in so many different ways and settings that at one time it was considered a mercy if you died in your own bed. The death rate was higher across the lifespan, and a hundred years ago it was a rare home that had not seen several coffins carried down the stairs. We still grieved and had broken hearts (over some more than others), but we knew what a corpse looked like because we washed and dressed and buried our own dead.

When you see a dead body, it is immediately clear that the soul, spirit, animating force, is gone. There is nothing stiller than a body whose spirit has departed, and no matter how well you recognize the face, there is an indefinable something missing—an energy. This body has no animation; you can move it, adjust its clothing, do anything at all to it, and it remains passive. This is why we speak of "dead weight" when we have to carry something that is utterly without buoyancy.

In India, there is a long tradition of spiritual practices that involve meditating on death. In a country where, to this day, many people lead their entire lives out of doors, death is an everyday reality, and culturally, people are disposed to at least try to come to terms with it. A famous story tells of a woman who came weeping to the Buddha, heartbroken by her child's death. "Bring her back to life," she begged, "because you can!"

"I can," agreed the Buddha, "and I will bring your daughter back to life, if you will bring me a measure of mustard seed from a house where no one has died." Naturally, the woman ran immediately to every house in the village, but in every single home, someone had died. By the time she returned to the Buddha empty-handed, the logic of her experience had begun to dawn, and she was able to accept the truth: We are of a nature to die. There is no escaping death.

When the world was first created, the creatures began to reproduce. Soon the world was full. Brahma, the creator, wondered where he had gone wrong. Sarasvati, the goddess of wisdom, told him, "You have no exit strategy. Souls have a way into the world, but not out. You must create Death!" So Brahma made Mrityu, a dark-skinned woman dressed in red. He ordered her to go out and take people's breath, end their lives. She was horrified and ran away. Shiva found her weeping.

He told her, "Don't be too sad. I will see to it that all who die are reborn; death will not be the end of all life, but the doorway from one life to another. You will be a killer, but a midwife also." Mrityu became Mahakali, the dark goddess who devours all life, and Shiva became Mahakala, the Lord of Time, the regenerator. Together they transform the ruins of one creation into the foundations for another.

Corpse Pose *(shavasana)*

Embodying the Pose

Lie flat on the floor, or on your mat. If your head falls back, place a folded blanket under the base of the skull; adjust so that the forehead is level with or slightly higher than the chin. Extend the legs fully, then let them go; keep the heels together and let the toes roll out naturally. Place the arms at the sides with the palms facing the ceiling. Find the midline of your body and make minute adjustments till you feel that your limbs are balanced on either side. Close the eyes. Place an eyebag or a dark cloth, folded several times, over the eyes. Release the jaw. Keep your tongue, eyes, and brain passive. Breathe deeply, but make the breath so fine and quiet that there is no sense of warm air/cool air passing through the nostrils. Relax completely. Remain here for 15 or 20 minutes.

Sustaining the Pose

Just be here. Notice the breath, notice the mind. When the mind begins to wander, bring it back to the breath. Notice the pause at the bottom of the exhalation. Let your attention be drawn into that pause; wait there for the next inhalation. Dip just below the surface of awareness. Gradually, your breath will become slower, and each individual breath may appear to arise as a wave forms in the ocean. First there is an almost imperceptible gathering of energy, then it begins to take on form and movement. At last the breath reaches the edge of your nostrils as the wave would reach the shore. Experience the feel of the breath as it enters, dual, through your two nostrils, then becomes part of your body, and at last exits, to become singular once more outside your body.

With each exhalation, drop the body deeper into the earth's support. Allow your consciousness to widen inside your skull; let your inner landscape be as vast as the ocean or sky. In this pose, it is as if you sink into the very ground of being that is Shiva, and from that inner vantage point of infinity, you watch each breath, each thought, each sensation arise and pass away.

A Meditation on Death From Father Joe Pereira

Think to yourself, as you lie in *shavasana*, that you are bidding farewell to everything that is important to you—your friends, your job, your home, finally, your body. Say to each thing mentally, "You are very precious to me, but you are not my life. I have a life to lead and a destiny to meet that are beyond you. Thank you, and good-bye." End this visualization with the image of meeting God and saying, "You are my life."

Releasing the Pose

Deepen the inhalation. Bend the knees. Roll to the side, and use your arms to roll back up to a seated position.

Points for Practice

Notice what happens when your body becomes perfectly still. At first, a thousand tiny physical sensations may demand notice. As you let go, progressively, of those claims on your attention, you may begin to notice what arises in the mind. When you hold your focus on the breath, the mental claims too will disperse, and eventually you will discover a silent, inner spaciousness—the background against which all thought and sensation arise.

Practice surrendering totally to the support of the floor. Where in your body or mind do you resist surrendering, resist accepting support? Search patiently for secret nests of tension. If it is uncomfortable for your lower back to lie flat, elevate the legs as much as necessary. If you have breathing problems lying flat, elevate the chest on a bolster; if you need assistance in getting comfortable, consult with an experienced teacher to help you find the right configuration of props.

Think: If you died now, would you be satisfied with the way you have lived?

Imagine your life really flowing out, so that you will get up to a new life. Are you at all reluctant to come back to life? To what or whom will you dedicate today's life?

How do you want to be remembered after death? As a loving person? An inspiring teacher? Someone who had great abs?

Journaling

Practice mentally, or in your journal, taking leave of everything you hold dear. Are these the things that make you afraid to die? Recall Shankaracharya's beautiful leave-taking prayer, which says, *I am not this, I am not that* . . . Shivo'ham. *I am Shiva.*

In the *Bhagavad Gita* (6.23), Lord Krishna suggests, "Let the dissolution of union with pain be called yoga." As we begin to perceive the suffering inherent in all attachments, the logic of experience leads us to let go. The surprise is, as we let go of our identification with pain, the more clearly our underlying, true nature reveals itself as infinite and eternal, and we say, with the conviction of experience, "I am Shiva."

May our yoga practice lead us all to this realization!

Bibliography

Anderson, Sandra and Rolf Sovik. *Yoga: Mastering the Basics*. Honesdale: Himalayan Institute Press, 2001.

Calasso, Roberto. *Ka: Stories of the Mind and Gods of India*. Trans. Tim Parks. New York: Vintage, 1999.

Cameron, Julia. *The Artist's Way*. New York: Tarcher, 2002.

Coulter, H. David. *Anatomy of Hatha Yoga: A Manual for Students, Teachers and Practitioners*. Honesdale: Body and Breath, 2001.

Goldberg, Natalie. *Wild Mind*. New York: Bantam, 1990.

———. *Writing Down the Bones: Freeing the Writer Within*. Boston: Shambhala, 2006.

Iyengar, B. K. S. *Light on Yoga*. New York: Shocken, 1995.

———. *Light on the Yoga Sutras of Patanjali*. New York: Thorsons, 2003.

Jung, C. G. and Robert A. Segal. *Jung on Mythology*. Princeton: Princeton University Press, 1998.

Kraftsow, Gary. *Yoga for Transformation: Ancient Teachings and Practices for Healing the Body, Mind, and Heart*. New York: Penguin, 2002.

Lasater, Judith. *Living Your Yoga: Finding the Spiritual in Everyday Life*. Berkeley: Rodmell Press, 2000.

———. *30 Essential Yoga Poses: For Beginning Students and Their Teachers*. Berkeley: Rodmell Press, 2003.

———. *A Year of Living Your Yoga: Daily Practices to Shape Your Life.* Berkeley: Rodmell Press, 2006.

Mishra, Rammurti (Sri Brahmananda Sarasvati). *Fundamentals of Yoga: A Handbook of Theory, Practice, and Application.* New York: Three Rivers Press, 1987.

Narayan, Kirin. *Storytellers, Saints, and Scoundrels: Folk Narrative in Hindu Religious Teaching.* Philadelphia: University of Pennsylvania Press, 1989.

O'Flaherty, Wendy Doniger. *Asceticism and Eroticism in the Mythology of Siva.* Oxford: Oxford University Press, 1973; retitled *Siva: The Erotic Ascetic.* New York: Galaxy, 1981.

———. *Dreams, Illusion, and Other Realities.* Chicago: University of Chicago Press, 1984.

———. *Hindu Myths: A Sourcebook, translated from the Sanskrit.* New York: Penguin Classics, 1975.

———. *Women, Androgynes, and Other Mythical Beasts.* Chicago: University of Chicago Press, 1980.

Olsen, Andrea. *Bodystories: A Guide to Experiential Anatomy.* Barrytown: Station Hill Press, 1991.

Radha, Swami Sivananda. *Hatha Yoga: The Hidden Language: Symbols, Secrets, and Metaphor.* Kootenay Bay, BC: Timeless Books, 2006.

Rama, Swami. *Perennial Psychology of the Bhagavad Gita.* Honesdale: Himalayan Institute Press, 1985.

Rig Veda, translated and edited by Wendy Doniger. New York: Penguin Classics, 2005.

Sparrowe, Linda and Patricia Walden. *The Woman's Book of Yoga &*
Health. Boston: Shambhala, 2002.

Svatmarama. *Hatha Yoga Pradipika, translated with commentary by*
Swami Muktibodhananda. Munger: Bihar School of Yoga, 1998.

Yoga Sutras of Patanjali: Commentary on the Raja Yoga Sutras by Sri
Swami Satchidananda. Yogaville: Integral Yoga Publications, 1990.

Acknowledgements

The artwork that illuminates this book is from author's personal collection. While most of it was created by unknown artists, we would like to acknowledge those whose identity is known.

Shiva Bhairava with dogs (page 51) by Kailash Raj
Gangavatara (page 67) and Markandeya (page 91) by Ravi Varma

All asana photos (pages 8, 14, 22, 28, 34, 40, 46, 52, 60, 68, 76, 84, 92, 100) © Himalayan Institute
Photo of Zo Newell (page 111) © Laura Goode Killmaster

We would also like to acknowledge Father Joe Pereira as the inspiration behind the Meditation on Death (page 104).

About the Author

Zo Newell was introduced to yoga by Dr. Rammurti S. Mishra (Sri Brahmananda Sarasvati) when she was fourteen. She earned her master of theological studies degree from Harvard Divinity School in 1988 and is currently working on a PhD in the history and critical theory of religion at Vanderbilt University. Zo lives in Nashville, Tennessee, where she teaches restorative yoga and yoga philosophy through the Yoga School. She is married and is the mother of three dogs.

THE HIMALAYAN INSTITUTE

The main building of the Institute headquarters near Honesdale, Pennsylvania

FOUNDED IN 1971 BY SWAMI RAMA, the Himalayan Institute has been dedicated to helping people grow physically, mentally, and spiritually by combining the best knowledge of both the East and the West.

Our international headquarters is located on a beautiful 400-acre campus in the rolling hills of the Pocono Mountains of northeastern Pennsylvania. The atmosphere here is one to foster growth, increase inner awareness, and promote calm. Our grounds provide a wonderfully peaceful and healthy setting for our seminars and extended programs. Students from all over the world join us here to attend programs in such diverse areas as hatha yoga, meditation, stress reduction, ayurveda, nutrition, Eastern philosophy, psychology, and other subjects. Whether the programs are for weekend meditation retreats, week-long seminars on spirituality, months-long residential programs, or holistic health services, the attempt here is to provide an environment of gentle inner progress. We invite you to join with us in the ongoing process of personal growth and development.

The Institute is a nonprofit organization. Your membership in the Institute helps to support its programs. Please call or write for information on becoming a member.

PROGRAMS AND SERVICES INCLUDE:

- Weekend or extended seminars and workshops
- Meditation retreats and advanced meditation instruction
- Hatha yoga teachers training
- Residential programs for self-development
- Holistic health services and pancha karma at the Institute's Center for Health and Healing
- Spiritual excursions
- Varcho Veda® herbal products
- Himalayan Institute Press
- *Yoga + Joyful Living* magazine
- Sanskrit Home Study course

A guide to programs and other offerings is free within the USA. To request a copy, or for further information, call 800-822-4547 or 570-253-5551, write to the Himalayan Institute, 952 Bethany Turnpike, Honesdale, PA 18431, USA; or visit our website at www.HimalayanInstitute.org.

HIMALAYAN INSTITUTE® PRESS

HIMALAYAN INSTITUTE PRESS has long been regarded as the resource for holistic living. We publish dozens of titles, as well as audio and videotapes that offer practical methods for living harmoniously and achieving inner balance. Our approach addresses the whole person—body, mind, and spirit—integrating the latest scientific knowledge with ancient healing and self-development techniques.

As such, we offer a wide array of titles on physical and psychological health and well-being, spiritual growth through meditation and other yogic practices, as well as translations of yogic scriptures.

Our yoga accessories include the Japa Kit for meditation practice and the Neti Pot™, the ideal tool for sinus and allergy sufferers. Our Varcho Veda® line of quality herbal extracts is now available to enhance balanced health and well-being.

Subscriptions are available to a bimonthly magazine, *Yoga + Joyful Living,* which offers thought-provoking articles on all aspects of meditation and yoga, including yoga's sister science, ayurveda.

For a free catalog, call 800-822-4547 or 570-253-5551; email hibooks@HimalayanInstitute.org; fax 570-647-1552; write to the Himalayan Institute Press, 952 Bethany Tpke., Honesdale, PA 18431, USA; or visit our website at www.HimalayanInstitute.org.